Ready for Love Now

Heather Morris

ACKNOWLEDGMENTS

Because this is the last book of the Colvin Series, I want to take this time to thank every single one of you who have read these books that I've spent so much time writing. I have loved to write this family's story and I pray you all have enjoyed reading them.

I would like to thank my grandmother Lill Penn for allowing me to use her artwork for the cover of this final book. My sister and aunt have also helped bring the Colvin Series covers to life and I couldn't be more proud to have them.

Thank you again, to Kristi Estes for typing the contents of the book for me from my scribblings. Without you I'd probably still be working on Chapter 3. You're much appreciated.

Lastly, thank you to my husband and girls. I'm sure you've lost out on time with me while I was in the writing mode and please know I love you always.

Chapter 1

"Glad you both could make it." Jonathan shakes Tarley and Carter's hands. He asked the two of them over to the house that Double B Construction has been working on the past couple of months.

"Of course. What's up? Everything okay?" Tarley asks with a worried look on his face. Poor guy always has that same expression all the time.

"Everything's fine. I just wanted to let you both know that I'm leaving you two in charge when Lizzie and I go on our honeymoon. Carter you will be in charge here and Tarley you will be in charge of Arianna until my mom and sister get back from Miami."

"You think that's wise? How long will that be?" Panic fills Tarley at the thought of playing daddy.

"Relax. It will only be for two days. Think you can handle it?"

"Um, I suppose so." Tarley is clearly not sure.

"You can always ask Monica for help. She's always great with Arianna when she's around her." Jonathan tries not to look at a very silent Carter standing there. He knows what face he's making without looking. Carter always shakes his head and rolls his eyes when Tarley and Monica are mentioned.

"Is that all you needed from me? I've got work to do." Carter finally says clearly angry. Jonathan nods his head and Carter walks off quickly; mumbling under his breath.

"He's going to hate you forever." Jonathan jokes and smacks Tarley on the shoulder.

"He doesn't bother me in the least. Are you sure about leaving me in charge of your daughter?"

"I'm sure. You two get along great."

"Yes when you're around. I've never dealt with her on my own! I don't know how to play Daddy."

"Calm down, it will be fine. Monica already said she would help out with anything you needed."

"You asked her before even asking me?"

"I knew you wouldn't say no but I wanted to make sure you had back-up."

"Aren't you a smart one?" Tarley glares and walks to the 6AB pick-up he has been using since taking the foreman position.

"Thanks man. Knew I could count on you!"

Tarley hears the words and throws his arms in the air. Boy that meeting went over well. Both men left the same way.

***

"I'm so tired of seeing and hearing about that big lug!"

"You're in a great mood tonight Carter, what's wrong now?" Maysen asks as Carter walks in the front door of Correli Repair.

"Jonathan called he and I into a meeting today and just had to bring her up. It's B.S."

"Dude, they've been hanging out for a couple of months now. Don't you think it's time to let your obsession with Monica go?" He says and gets an immediate glare from Carter.

"I don't know what she sees in him that she doesn't see in me! He's just a big dumb idiot!"

"Carter he is, was, a U.S. Army soldier. He isn't a big dumb idiot. He's actually pretty cool." Maysen says knowing Carter is going to throw a fit.

"What? You're his girlfriend now too?"

"Oh grow up man. He's a decent guy and I like him. And furthermore, he is my father-in-law's foreman remember? I kinda have to talk to the guy at times."

"I know but I don't have to love the guy. He's totally wrong for Monica and one of these days she's going to realize what she's missing."

"Oh I'm sure she will once you stop sleeping with every available girl in the neighboring three counties!"

"She doesn't need to know that much. Those girls are just keeping me company until the love of my life comes around."

"You're so delusional dude. Are you even listening to yourself?" Shaking his head at Carter.

"Don't shake your head at me. You'll see, one of these days soon she's going to see what has been right in front of her this entire time." With that Carter walks out of Maysen's shop and to his car eager to text tonight's girl.

"Maysen doesn't know what he's talking about."

Chapter 2

"Monica did the electrician ever make it to your house last week and look at those switches?" Aaron asks before leaving the office for the day.

"No, he called and said he would have to do it this week, but Tarley changed them out for me so we're all good."

"Your knight in shining armor." He says and bumps her arm wearing a big smile from ear to ear.

"He's a great friend, yes. Nothing more. I've been telling you and everyone else that for months."

"None of us believe it, you know?"

"I couldn't tell." She says sarcastically and rolls her eyes.

"Maybe we all see something that you don't."

"I see the same things everyone else does, I'm just not ready for a relationship."

"What are you afraid of Mon? Are you waiting for Carter to change his womanizing ways?" That obnoxious grin.

"Hardly. I'm afraid of losing myself and all I've worked for."

"What are you talking about?" Aaron is clearly dumbfounded.

"I've worked so hard to be a strong and independent woman living in a man's world. If everyone sees that I'm leaning on a man, they'll all perceive me as weak again."

"Whoa girl. You have messed up views of the world. Amie is a woman and she's far from weak. Same with Karlie, Leah, Lizzie and even my mother."

"Yes I know, but they're exceptions to the rule. They have amazing men who love that side of them and don't try to change them."

6

"And you're saying Tarley will make you change who you are? I don't believe that for a second. He seems like the kind of guy that would want a strong and independent woman. Hate to break it to you but most men don't like the weak and clingy women you're envisioning."

"Maybe not in your perfect little world but I saw the women you went through before you met Amie."

"Is that where you got this idea from? I was not looking for anything past the one night with those women. But once I met Amie those ideals changed and I wouldn't want her any other way."

"I know. I really do. I'm just not willing to be someone's 'right now'. I will hold out until I find the one that wants me just the way I am, forever."

"What makes you think you haven't found him?"

"Aaron. Listen to me, please. I'm not ready for a relationship with Tarley or anyone right now. If I was I probably would have given that womanizing Carter a chance a long time ago. Ok?"

"Alright I'll back off. Just promise me you'll be open and honest with yourself where Tarley is concerned."

"Deal. Now get out of here. Isn't your wife expecting you for some secret meeting?" I smile and wink at Aaron.

"Secret meeting? What are you talking about now?"

"You're so obtuse. Just go. We'll talk later." I shake my head as he walks out the door.

I think Amie is going to tell him at lunch that she's pregnant but that's just me thinking out loud. I could be way off base but she sure seems different to me. Time will tell.

About an hour later the door swings open to the portable trailer we have set up on the current job site. I use it as my office and Aaron holds employee meetings here too sometimes.

I look up expecting to see an ecstatic Aaron but find Tarley instead.

"Well, hello there. What are you doing in town in the middle of the day?"

"Jonathan asked me to come in. He wanted a meeting with me and your lover boy." He smiles mischievously and I choose to ignore that comment.

"Why both of you? I bet that went over well."

"Just as you imagine." Tarley says and sits in a chair across from my desk. I look closer at him and he's smiling.

"What are you so cheesy for?"

"Just makes me laugh how much that guy wants you and how much you don't want him. You do stand firm on not wanting him, right?"

"It's not funny. It's annoying. I don't know what it's going to take to get him to forget about his little school boy crush."

"Go out with me tonight."

"Yea because that would help. He practically has a hissy fit anytime your name is even mentioned, let alone seeing us talking." I roll my eyes and try to ignore the thoughts rolling around in the back of my head. If only he was really asking me out. But how would I feel about that? Damn you Aaron for putting these thoughts in my head.

"There's only one way to find out." He's looking straight at me and wants a real answer.

"You cannot be serious. Are you serious?" I'm thoroughly confused now.

"We've been getting to know each other for several months now. I'd like to get to know another side of you." He smiles. Thank goodness he smiled and made this all less awkward. Geez.

"You're serious. Um, sure I guess." Crap, Aaron was right.

"You guess? If you're not interested in anything more than friendship Monica, you need to tell me now."

"Um, you know how I feel about dating. I'm so afraid Tarley."

"Monica, just trust me this once, ok?"

"Ok, but I can't promise you anything more." I'm so uncomfortable right now and unable to look him in the eyes. This is a great start.

"Quit looking at your desk and look at me Monica. I can't guarantee that I'm ready for more either. I do know that I love spending time with you and I'm always thinking about you."

"Really? I never would have guessed you liked having me as a friend that much." Hmm interesting.

"I think I want you to be more than a friend though. The only way to be sure is to try it. Right?"

"Um I guess? Tarley do you have any idea how scared I am right now? I see him stand up and walk around to my side of the desk. That desk was my shield, what's he doing?

"Monica, I know you're scared and heck, so am I. We'll do this together. Baby steps."

"Baby steps. Ok. I can do that." He leans over and pulls me up to my feet and gives me a big hug. This is new and I've got to admit that it feels pretty great. Maybe I can do this after all. Maybe.

"Speaking of babies." I jerk out of his embrace.

"Who was talking about babies? Good grief I only meant I would…." Tarley's hand flies over my mouth stopping the rest of my tirade. I look up at him to find he's amused beyond measure.

"Calm down. I was only meaning that I had something I forgot to tell you about Jonathan's baby."

"She's not a baby, Tarley."

"I know but I'm not exactly an expert on tiny humans. Anyway, the reason he wanted to meet with me today was to tell me I was babysitting a few days when they leave on their honeymoon."

"You? What about Karlie or Ella Mae?"

"My first thought too but I guess they will be gone and I will keep her, I mean we will keep her until they return."

"We?"

"I was hoping you would help me. You're so good with her. And Jonathan said you already agreed."

"When she's with her parents! I don't know any more than you do about babies. I don't recall agreeing to play mommy."

"You already said she's not a baby. And you won't be mommy."

"Oh brother! You're not going to let me out of this are you? I didn't think Jonathan was serious."

"Please stay with me at Ella Mae's those days and help me? I really need back up." He pulls me in for another hug making it even more difficult to tell him no with the way my heart is racing.

"Fine. The wedding is not for a few weeks so maybe we better get more Arianna time while her parents are nearby." I step out of his arms needing to clear my head before I start stuttering.

"See, this is why I need you. You're so smart and keep me on my toes. Be ready at 6."

And out he goes making this trailer feel vast and empty.

What have I agreed to?

Chapter 3

"Zandra this is so hard to do over video chat. Why can't you just hop on Daddy's jet and come help me in person?" Lizzie whines while trying to pick out flowers for her wedding at Stampley's. I hear Leah carrying on about each flower Lizzie touches.

"I don't think he'll be ok with that."

"Do you know how stupid I look standing in this sea of flowers talking to my phone? Everyone is looking at me." She looks around to find no one is actually there except Leah but she won't tell her friend that.

"You're lying but I forgive you. There aren't enough people in that small town to worry me. I will talk to Daddy and see what he says. He's pressuring me to help his newest wife with her new clothing store but I really don't want to."

"Zandra you really need to tell him you want to open up a bridal boutique. I don't understand why you're so scared to tell him."

"You know my father. He pours money into anything his wives want to do but makes me work for it. I don't want to help step-mommy sell her ugly clothes. Maybe I do need a break."

"Yes you do. I'll pick you up in Tulsa if you'll come help me. I've saved the dress for last anyway."

"I still can't believe you don't have a dress yet. Most brides get those the day after the man pops the question."

"I'm doing it my own way."

"No, you've been hoping I would come rescue you."

"Maybe."

"Ok, I'll come. Let me get packed and go talk to Daddy. If he doesn't kill me, I will see you tonight!"

"Let me know your flight information! Cannot wait to see you! You're a lifesaver!"

"Yea, yea, yea. He's going to kill me. You know that right?"

"Nah, see you soon!" Lizzie hangs up leaving Zandra with quite a predicament.

"Well, it's now or never." She gets up and heads to her closet to pack.

***

"Hey Carter, why don't you come with us to Tulsa tonight to pick up Lizzie's friend Zandra?"

"Jonathan, I don't need babysat. You're my boss here but once I punch that time clock you and I don't know each other."

"Wow, what has got you so cranky today?"

"Seriously? Your little double meeting today with your BFF? Ring a bell?"

"Why do you hate Tarley so much? He's a great guy. I think you would like him if you gave him a chance."

"Spare me. I will never get along with that big lug."

"You do realize that she's not yours and he didn't steal her from you?"

"Shut up! I'm not having this conversation again! I've already heard it from Maysen every day since I met her."

"Why are you so obsessed with her? You have been with every available woman in a fifty-mile radius. Why this one who is clearly not interested?"

"I said, I'm not doing this!" And Carter storms off leaving Jonathan shaking his head.

"Who does he think he is? He doesn't know me! We are not even friends! Why would I want to ride an hour in a car with him and his new happy family to pick up some chick? No thank you!"

I start my pick up and head to the only place I can think of that I won't hear about how unhealthy my obsession is with Monica. The Bar. I smile at the sign as I pull up in front. It really is called "The Bar".

"Someone was clever." I turn off the ignition and lean my head back. I've got to get a hold of myself before I go inside and knock someone out that looks at me wrong.

"Hey Carter. Your normal?" Louie the bartender asks as I walk up to the counter and take a seat on the nearest stool.

"Please. I need about twenty to wash the past couple of months away."

"Monica again?" Louie asks trying to be sympathetic.

"You know it." Dang, this whole situation makes me so mad! And everyone else thinks they know what I should and shouldn't be doing. Or feeling.

Chapter 4

I awake quickly to the sound of my phone ringing. The plane I'm on is about to take off from the Charlotte airport heading for Tulsa.

"Hello Daddy." I hit answer and say knowing this is not going to be good.

"Where on Earth do you think you're going young lady? Your mother and I are counting on your help at the boutique." I roll my eyes at that.

"She's not my mother. I'm going to Oklahoma to help Lizzie plan her wedding. I lined up other help for the boutique before I left."

"We need you Zandra. We pay you to take care of it all."

"I know Daddy but I need to go help my friend and to be honest your new store is ready to open. There's really nothing else that needs to be done on my end."

"So you're going on a mini-vacation as we open? I thought our expectations were clear when we decided to open this boutique."

"Daddy this is her baby, not mine. If you would let me open the bridal store I would be a lot more invested. But you won't even have a conversation about what I would like to do, will you?"

"You need to watch your tone young lady. I'm still your father regardless of your age."

"I know, I'm sorry. I just need a little time to breathe and I'll come back to help however I can."

"Why are you not on the jet? You could have asked me. You didn't need to fly commercial."

"Daddy I'm still in 1st class but it's honestly not that bad. And I bought a ticket so I didn't have to bother you for the jet."

"Let me know when you're ready to come back to Charlotte. I'll have the jet there to bring you home."

"Okay Daddy, Love you."

"Keep me posted on your arrival."

"Bye." I hang up and breathe in deep. That went much better than I anticipated. Whew.

On the plane. See you soon.

I text Lizzie quickly before they tell me to shut off all electronic devices. Now back to my little nap.

****

"Carter. Earth to Carter." I snap out of my alcohol induced hangover to look up at Lizzie standing before me.

"What do you want? You can see your hubby's not here right now." I scowl up at her very smiley face. Good grief what's there to be so happy about?

"I came to talk to you. I can see you're in a great mood today. Have a wild night again?" This time she scowls at me.

"Not wild no. Just a lot of alcohol. What?"

"Are you ever going to grow up? Quit drinking and sleeping with any female that will give you a second glance?"

"What are you? My mother?" She rolls her eyes at me but doesn't leave me alone like I had hoped for.

"You're such a pig and a child. I wanted to invite you over tonight to meet my friend who is on her way right now. But if you're in this foul of a mood never mind." Now she chooses to storm off.

Later that day, I'm feeling like a total jerk. She was only trying to be nice and I had to be awful. Jonathan might kick my butt for this one. I take out my phone and text him.

Please tell Lizzie I'm sorry and I would love to come. I'm a jerk.

Didn't have to wait very long for an answer back from him.

Yes, you are. See you at 6:30.

Wonderful. I really don't want to be part of some big reunion but I need to make it up to Lizzie. Let's hope Jonathan didn't invite anyone in particular. Surely they know better than to put us all under one roof and at one table. At the same time. Please no.

Chapter 5

I cannot believe I'm going on a date tonight with Tarley. Oh crap, I don't know what to expect and my heart is racing so fast. I might have a heart attack before he even gets here.

"Breathe Monica. He's your friend and you know you like him as more than a friend. Just breathe and relax. Tarley will happen as God intended." Looking in the full length mirror I realize it has been a long time since I last felt this nervous about a date. Heck it has been a long time since my last date.

"That makes you sound pathetic. Good thing you don't have fifteen cats or you would be the grumpy cat lady."

I cannot let myself end up like that. I had the same fairy tale dream in my head growing up that every other little girl had. That was until I realized what the world is like for a girl with those dreams.

"That doesn't mean Tarley is like that. You know him and you know he's a strong willed man with his own things to deal with."

I look at myself one more time in the mirror and laugh.

"You're carrying on a conversation with yourself. You clearly need to get a life and maybe even a man."

Shaking my head, I walk towards the living room knowing the door bell is going to ring any second.

Ding Dong.

Yep there it is. No turning back now. Deep breath. Maybe another for safe measures.

***

I pull up in front of Monica's house and the circus going on inside my gut is unnerving. I know it has been a very long time since my last date but good grief. I feel like a teenager going on his first date. My palms are

Heather Morris

sweaty, my heart is racing and I feel like I might throw up.

"Man up! You have known her long enough what's the big deal?" I smack myself on the cheeks hoping to knock some sense into me.

"Here goes nothing." I get out of my pick up, well my work pickup, and walk to her door.

As I get closer, the circus performance dies down and a strange calmness washes over me. One last deep breath and I push the doorbell. I cannot wait to see her beautiful face. Ok, part of me also cannot wait to see what she has on too.

"Enough loser. Get your head on straight." Just as I finish that line she opens the door and catches me talking to myself.

"Guilty." Oh my goodness she looks like a dream come true!

Did I seriously just say that? What has gotten into me? I'm going soft just like Jonathan. I'm not sure how I feel about this!

"You look amazing Monica. I love that dress."

"You clean up nicely yourself. You even wore a tie. I feel so special." That smile kills me every time.

"Why thank you. You should feel special because I don't even own a tie."

"Jonathan?"

"Yes, Lizzie made sure I looked hot so she picked it out. "I smile at her understanding now why Lizzie was so adamant about the clothes. The look of approval on Monica's face makes the ten clothing changes I had to endure worth it.

"Well, you do look hot." She looks down at her hands as she says that and turns a few shades of red. She's even more beautiful when she's embarrassed.

"Are you ready for our date?" I reach out my hand for her in hopes she

18

will take it.

The universe is on my side tonight as she shuts the front door and slips her dainty little hand into my large one.

Fireworks sizzling between our skin would be an understatement. I thought my heart was racing before.... Wow. This is really happening.

Chapter 6

"Carter. Thanks for coming. I hope you're in a better mood than you were earlier." Jonathan says when opening their front door.

"Apologize for being cranky?" We hear Lizzie's voice come from another room.

Jonathan opens the door all the way allowing me to step inside. He motions towards a doorway where we can hear two women laughing.

"Ready for this? She is a handful just like you." I hear him say as I walk to the doorway. Before I walk in I turn and glare at him. I am not a handful.

"Yes, I need to apologize for being in such a bad mood earlier today. You didn't deserve it and I truly am sorry." I put my right hand on my chest over where my heart is.

"All forgiven." Lizzie gives me a hug and as I put my arms around her waist to reciprocate, I see the look on Jonathan's face. I smile wide and pull her close. I think his face just turned four shades of red before walking up and pulling her out of my arms.

"Ok Casanova, this one is taken." I smile and step back. I cannot help but feel a little pang of envy for what they have.

"Carter, I wanted to introduce you to my best friend from Charlotte. She's here to help with the wedding. Zandra, this is Carter. Carter this is Zandra." I think I just stepped out of the real world and into a dream world I've never heard of.

The most beautiful woman I've ever seen steps out from behind Lizzie with a smile that could light up a room. She has got light chocolate skin, jet black long hair and eyes so dark I could get lost in them.

"Carter! What's wrong with you?" I feel Jonathan hit me on the back of the head as I come out of my daze.

"I'm sorry, I'm an idiot. It is very nice to meet you. Zandra is such an unusual name. It is beautiful just like you." I smile and extend my hand when she sets her hand in mine I lift it and gently place my lips against the top of her hand.

"You are a player aren't you?" She pulls her hand back with a look of disgust on her face.

"I see they have told you all about me before I got here. Not fair. Don't believe everything they say."

"Oh she definitely needs to listen to everything we have said." Jonathan says and grabs me by the arm pulling me into the other room.

"I was just being friendly." I smile knowing full well that I had the charm turned up to 100.

"I know. She's not going to be another one of your conquests. I'm serious." Wow, by the look on his face you would think she was his little sister.

"I simply said hello and kissed her hand. I didn't seduce her." Yet.

"Yet." Shocked to hear him say exactly what I was thinking. I look at him quickly to see a knowing look on his face.

"Okay I get it. Hands off that smoking hot woman in your kitchen. Why did you invite me here tonight then?" I put my hands up in surrender but he's not fooled.

"Hands and every other part of you especially those googly eyes you had back there!"

I laugh. "You sound like you're thirteen."

"Whatever, I mean it. Let's watch the game."

I sit down on the other end of the sofa. I cannot quit thinking of Zandra in the other room. I need to find another woman. Another one? Is that not what they all have told me about Monica? What's wrong with me? Every woman is off limits around here!

"You look like you're about to explode, what's wrong with you tonight?"

"Oh, um, I was thinking."

"Well don't hurt yourself."

"You're funny. Let's watch the game." I don't like this uneasy feeling.

***

"He's cute Liz. Why is he off limits again?"

"Zandra trust me he's not someone you want to get involved with. We have told you all about how he is."

"Maybe I want someone with no strings."

"You? Seriously? I thought you wanted someone who could get your dad off your back?"

"And that hunk of man candy in there couldn't?"

"I should not have invited him over here."

"It is fine. I'm a big girl but I honestly don't have time while I'm here anyway."

"True. You're here to help me with this wedding."

"Yes. Speaking of, who is going to be the best man?" I wiggle my eyebrows making her laugh out loud.

"Not Carter. It is actually his least favorite person. Long story. Jonathan's best friend from the Army is his best man. Tarley."

"Oh yeah, duh. I knew that."

"You thought you would get to walk down with Carter. You're going to make me regret asking you to come to Colvin aren't you?" She smiles knowing exactly what's going to happen with me and Carter. Well, what I hope will happen anyway.

"Let's eat!" Lizzie calls and the guys come in and Jonathan looks at Carter like he's warning him to behave. I get the same look from Lizzie and smile back. She can warn me all she wants; I don't have time for him anyway.

Chapter 7

"Where are we going? Surely you're not going to make Amelia cook for us?" I look over at Tarley completely confused. It looks like we are heading to the 6AB.

"Ye of little faith." A smile. Hmmm. My goodness he's extra handsome all cleaned up.

Ten minutes later we do turn onto the driveway of the Blake family ranch. I know he's the foreman but really?

Tarley pulls up to the front of the main house and gets out without saying a word to me. I see him walk inside and I'm left sitting in his pickup. Alone.

"This has to be the worst start to a date I've ever had." I grunt and cross my arms over my chest.

I'm so mad. I should have known this was a bad idea. I should have left things the way they were! Hmph!

Before I can finish my hissy fit I catch sight of Tarley coming back out of the house carrying a large picnic basket. A picnic basket, how sweet.

I'm immediately filled with shame because of where my thoughts were going. He has the biggest smile on his face as he gets in the cab after setting the basket in the bed of the pickup.

"Ok, now are you ready for dinner?" That smile I'll never get used to melts my insides.

"I am." I feel so horrible for doubting him. I don't deserve him, that's for sure.

***

"I know you're probably wondering where we are having dinner." I say and look over at Monica. Her face is red but I'm not sure why. What did I do now?

"I am, yes." She looks away from me too quickly. Yep, she's definitely mad at me.

"What's wrong?" I reach my right hand over and try to hold hers but she moves it away. Oh boy.

"Nothing. Are we almost there?" Now she's changing the subject.

"Did you think I was taking you to Amelia's for dinner?"

"I didn't know what you were doing." Oh, duh you moron.

"Oh crap. I didn't tell you I would be right back did I? I'm such an idiot." I slap my hand on my forehead like the idiot I am.

"You're not an idiot. I am for doubting you."

"Ok we are a pair of idiots. Glad we got that out in the open!" I laugh and feel much better when I hear her also chuckle.

"I'm so nervous about this whole thing and let my imagination run away with me."

"Well, we are here so let's start over." I get out of the pickup and walk to her door.

She looks over at me with such an angelic look on her face. I open her door and extend my hand for hers. To my relief, she puts it in mine and steps out of the pickup with a smile on her face. That's more like it.

"We are going this way." I point to the left where I pray she cannot see the table yet. I entwine my fingers with hers and lead her to where I've gotten everything set up. I hope she appreciates it all. Oh boy. Moment of truth.

***

Walking along this pathway has every nerve in my system on high alert. The butterflies are flying all over in my stomach and my hand has to be all sweaty inside of Tarley's. Oh my goodness this is all too much. I think I might pass out before we get wherever it is we are going.

"Almost there. I promise." I hear his deep voice say making the butterflies even more active. Holy cow, I need to sit down before I fall flat on my face. That would be attractive.

We turn right past a row of trees and I about faint at the sight. Tarley has a table and two chairs sitting inside a circle of at least a hundred candles. There are plates and silverware there that catch the glow of the candles and champagne flutes full of bubbly. Somewhere there is soft music playing too.

"Oh my goodness." I gasp. No other words would come out. How do I put words to this feeling I've got inside of me?

"Do you like it? Or is it too much? We can go somewhere else if you don't like it." Poor guy thinks I don't like this amazing display of everything romantic.

"Tarley this is the most amazing thing I've ever seen. I cannot believe you did all this. For me, no less." I've moved in front of him taking his other hand in mine. I see the doubt and fear written all over his face.

"Really? You like it?" I take a step closer to him and lay my head on his chest. I don't have a clue of how to show him just how touched I am with all this he has done for me.

"I don't like it. I love it. Absolutely love it. How could I not?" He takes his hands out of mine and wraps his arms around me allowing me to do the same.

Before I know it we are swaying to the beat of the music fully content with no words and only the feeling of each other's arms. I can hear his heart beat and love how fast it is going every time I squeeze a little tighter to him. Great to know he's as affected as I am.

Best. Night. Ever. We are about to hit fairy tale status.

Chapter 8

"Dude, you didn't tell me she was so hot."

"We all got that impression from the way you were ogling her last night. It was embarrassing."

"Oh Johnny-boy, I seem to remember hearing you go on and on about a smoking hot aunt some time ago." I raise one eyebrow and smirk at him.

"Touché. Still, you looked at her like she was a piece of meat. Lizzie was furious with you."

"Yea right. I heard them whispering like little girls in the kitchen." I laugh which makes Jonathan laugh too because he was trying his hardest to be stern about Zandra.

"I know. I was just trying to give you a hard time. You were pretty obvious though."

"I couldn't help it man. She is gorgeous. Nothing like any woman I've ever seen before in my life. Honest."

"Her daddy owns half of North Carolina too."

"Hot damn I hit the jackpot!"

"You're such a pig."

"I'm only joking. I'm not that big of a jerk." I'm really not but it's not like anyone would agree.

"Yea, sure you aren't. Can we get some work done now Romeo?"

"Slave driver." And off I go to get busy but a certain woman never leaves my thoughts. And it's not the one that normally takes up residence there.

"What shade of blue were you wanting for the bridal party?"

***

"Zandra that's what I need you for. You tell me. You're the expert here."

"An expert that's never actually walked down the aisle herself."

"Don't look at me like I've got horns coming out of my head. You know what I mean."

"Just because I want to open my own bridal shop doesn't make me an expert."

"You have been designing dresses since you were five."

"Okay, okay. I think you should do royal blue. It is classy and not one of the shades everyone else uses. I think it'll be timeless."

"Love it!" She smiles and leaves the room giving me that 'I told you so' look. I think I will ignore it though. Her head gets any bigger and she will have to get a different head piece.

"What are you smiling about over there?" I hear from beside me. I look over and see that Ella Mae has come into the kitchen.

"Just visualizing Lizzie with a gigantic head." We both laugh.

"So did you two decide on a color for all of us to wear? I need to start looking for my dress. Actually I might do that next week while we are in Miami."

"If you find a style you like I would be happy to make it for you. I'm making the other bridal party dresses. Oh, and Arianna's."

"I will let you know what I find. With all your other work I'm sure you have more than enough to do."

"You might be right. If you cannot find one, we will design you one just the way you like."

"Deal. Ok I'm off to the shop. Tell Lizzie I will see her later."

"What did Ella Mae want?" Lizzie asks coming back from putting Arianna down for a nap.

"I guess to ask about a dress color? I'm not sure."

"We need to find her a house. She has been renting the room I had at the B & B when I first came to Colvin."

"Wow. You kicked the poor woman out of her own house?"

"Shut up! I already feel terrible but Jonathan always says she likes the B & B. I don't know. I really do feel terrible though."

"So, next week when you go to Miami I think I will go home and talk to Dad about my shop."

"Finally. I don't know why he would say no. You're so good at this stuff! Look at what's been accomplished since you got here."

"Fingers crossed." Wish it were that easy. I know deep down it's a total waste of my time but I've got to at least say I tried, right?

Chapter 9

"Carter?" I hear when I answer my phone a couple of days later. I smile instantly as I recognize the voice on the other end.

"Monica. I knew you would come crawling back sooner or later."

"You're such a pig. I'm calling to tell you that the Stark jobsite had a water leak last night and we need you to go fix it."

"Oh. Sure. That's all you called me for?"

"Yes idiot." She hung up on me. Not cool, not cool at all. I should feel a lot more disappointment but oddly I don't. This is new.

I head over to the Stark house and see that Aaron has beat me there. Must be bad if the big boss is here.

"Hey man. What have we got?" I say to him when he looks up at me from the floor where he's crouched down looking at the busted pipe.

"Looks like it got hit by the delivery guys when they brought in all the dry wall."

"Yep. I would have fixed it already but my wife has my pickup which has all my tools in it."

"I will have it done in no time."

"That's why Monica called you."

"Yes, I found that out. She really does despise me doesn't she?" Why do I even ask, I know she does.

"Yes, she does. But I'm hearing talk about a new woman in town?"

"Oh you must mean Zandra. She's Lizzie's BFF and man is she smokin'!"

"I heard you took quite a liking to each other at dinner." Oh did he now?

"Oh you did, did you? Hmmm." I smile and wiggle my eyebrows.

"Poor girl doesn't have a chance does she?" He laughs and walks out the door.

So she likes me too? I'm thinking I need to make a stop by Jonathan's after work.

**

As soon as I enter the airplane owned by my father I feel the uneasy vibes. I look over at the seats knowing full well I'm going to see him sitting there drinking two fingers deep of scotch.

"Hello Daddy. What do I owe this surprise?" I ask sitting down across from him and buckling up. This is going to be a bumpy ride but I'm not talking about the airplane.

"Well, darling girl, I got word you requested a flight home so I thought it would be a great time for us to chat uninterrupted."

I let out a big sigh. "About what this time? What does her Highness want me to do now?"

"She has a name Zandra. You need to learn to respect my wife."

"I'm not having this conversation with you again Dad. Please just get to the point."

"Fine. We are selling the store and opening up a travel agency."

"Oh my goodness, seriously? She's bored already? It hasn't even opened yet."

"She's not bored she just doesn't feel adequate with the boutique. Since she loves to travel the agency would be perfect for her."

"And what does this have to do with me exactly?"

"We are going to need someone to answer the phones and keep the office tasks up."

"I wont be her little secretary Dad!"

"Why not? You're so good with people and she will need someone she can trust running the minor details on a day to day basis."

"I went to fashion design school in New York. I also have my bachelor's in business administration. I'm over qualified to answer phones for your wife."

"You think you're too good to help your family now? I see you got tired of being a big fish in that small town pond and came rushing back."

"Actually, Lizzie went out of town for a couple of days and I thought it would be a good chance to come say hello to my father."

"What else do you want? I know you. You're fighting me on this job because you have something else in mind." Dang he's good. Too good.

"You're right. There is something I wanted to talk to you about."

"Imagine that. How much is this going to cost me?"

"Nothing if you would just let me have my trust fund."

"Your grandfather set that up for you but you cannot have it until you're thirty years old. Last I checked you were a few years short of that."

"Dad, I'm fully aware that I cannot have it until you say so or I turn thirty. But there is a business venture I'm very passionate about. Will you at least hear me out?"

"Fine. You have until we land." Wow that's like ten minutes. Oh well, here goes nothing.

"So as you're well aware, I've been drawing and designing wedding dresses and bridal party dresses since I was five. I'm really good at it and have helped a lot of women through the years. Lizzie asked me to come help her because there is not anywhere close to them where they can get services like that except the big city. So I thought a lot about it and I want to open my own bridal salon. There is a party planning business that expressed interest in my salon too so I would have clients right away."

"And you think that little one horse town is going to be able to support a high end bridal salon?" The disapproval is so clear on his face that it makes my stomach hurt. I knew he would say no, why did I waste my breath?

"I do. The nearest place is in Tulsa which is an hour away. I could have the only salon serving the smaller areas around Colvin."

"Never going to happen. I'm not throwing my money away like that. You're needed here at the agency anyway."

"Are you serious? You cannot even do the research before you answer?"

"I don't need to. No child of mine is going to live in that small town and run a piddly store. Not when you're needed here."

"I cannot believe this! No, actually I can believe it!" My whole dream just shattered into a million pieces and he acts like it is no big deal and was just some stupid idea. I know I could make this work and I know it is what I want to do. But how do I do it without him or his approval? Okay and his money if I'm being honest. I cannot wait until I'm thirty to start this. Someone else will do it by then.   What do I do now?

***

"What are you doing here Carter?" Jonathan asks as he opens the front door.

"Just stopping by to say hello."

"Um hi. That happens so often. Let me guess you came hoping to see Zandra?" He raises one eyebrow and smirks.

"Maybe. But I also wanted to say I was sorry to Lizzie about how I acted at dinner the other night."

"Neither one is here. Lizzie and Mom went to Miami while Zandra went home."

"Home? Really? That quick? I didn't even get to really talk to her.

Dang." My whole plan is ruined now. Should have known it was all too good to be true.

"She's coming back loser." He rolls his eyes at me and shuts the door in my face. Well, that didn't quite work out as planned. I hope she does come back.

Chapter 10

"Tarley? How did your date with Monica go the other night? She like the set up?" Amelia asks me as I enter her kitchen for lunch with the other ranch hands.

"She did, yes. Thank you so much for your help. She said it was the most amazing thing she had ever seen." I smile a smile wider than my face wanted to allow.

"I'm so glad. Now that all of my kids are married I've gotten out of the matchmaking business but was so happy to jump back in with you and that sweet girl. You let me know if I can help with anything else."

"Oh boy you have got your hands full with her now." Aiden says coming in for lunch too.

"I can handle her."

"Ha! She used to drive all of us crazy until we found our spouses. She won't rest until she's gotten you married off like the rest of us."

"What have I done? Why did you not warn me before hand?" We all laugh knowing this is exactly the way to go.

***

"So? How was it? Aaron won't ask you but I have to know." Amie asks while walking into the trailer.

I look up and smile knowing that I've been waiting on this visit since the date happened.

Just as I was about to tell her all the juicy details, we hear the door open again and see the other three Blake girls show up.

"Let me guess, Leah, Karlie, Audrey and Amie, you all are here for the same reason?" They are all standing there like cats that ate the canaries.

"Well, this is the juiciest story we have had in a while." Leah says and the others murmur in agreement.

"How did you all find out anyway?" I don't think even Aaron knew.

"Mom told me and I might have called the others." Audrey says blushing.

"And Aaron told me." He did know? Crap.

"Well? We are dying to hear all about it. Lizzie and Zandra want to know too." Karlie says with a grin. I tell the story to 'oohs and aahs' and lots of smiles. I feel so giddy about it myself. It feels so good having girlfriends to talk about "boys" with again.

***

Knock. Knock.

I open the trailer door making sure the bouquet covered my face as I entered.

"Wow, who are those for?" I hear Monica ask as she stands up and comes towards me.

"Monica. Are you Monica?" I ask trying to disguise my voice.

"Yes, I am. Who on Earth could these be from? Actually there could be several men they could be from. Let me look at the card." I feel her grab the card and open the envelope. Several men? Seriously?

"I had an amazing time with you the other night. Hmm that still doesn't narrow it down and no one signed the card." What?

"Seriously?" I lower the flowers and ask with a little too much emotion. How can she not know they were from me? I know she's too good for the likes of me but good grief I didn't know she was dating others. Dang, this didn't go how I had hoped.

"Hello handsome." She stands there smiling ear to ear.

"Is that what you say to every suitor who brings you flowers?" I'm none too happy right now.

"I knew it was you the whole time Tarley."

"Wait? What? How did you know? All of that was fake?"

"Yes silly. I knew it was you because Austin and Leah do their own deliveries. And you're the only man who is ten feet tall and has to duck when coming in my door. Plus, your cologne gave you away." She's smiling again from ear to ear. That beautiful face makes my stomach do flips.

"You really had me going. I was getting a little hot under the collar." I look down at the floor and hand the flowers to her.

"I know. You had steam coming from your ears. Cruel joke. I'm sorry." She sets the flowers down and steps close to me. She looks up at me with a look on her face that makes my knees go weak.

I close the gap between us and wrap my arms around her waist. She sighs as I pull her up against me. This woman makes me feel things I never knew I could feel. Never dreamed I would feel.

***

When Tarley finally presses his lips to mine I feel like I'm going to implode. I love everything about this man and it scares the daylights out of me.

"You thought I was serious about the other men?" I say and snuggle into his chest. It is scary how good it feels to be wrapped up in his arms.

"I'm ashamed to say yes." If I didn't know better, I would think he just blushed a little. Poor guy.

"I wont tease you like that again. I promise." And I lift up to kiss him again.

"Promise sealed with a kiss. It is binding now." Hearing him chuckle makes the nerves inside me ease up. I really messed up that joke and made him second guess me. Smooth move dummy.

"I like those terms." I steal another kiss and it hits me that we have gone way past friends.

"Way past the fired zone now babe." I'm shocked to hear Tarley thinking the same thing I am.

"All the girls were here a while ago getting all the details. Talk of the town now."

"I'm oddly okay with that." Another kiss. This one leaves me breathless. I could so get used to this!

***

"So, do you wanna make it official or go on a few more dates before making that decision?" Jonathan asks me at home that night. I look over at him holding Arianna who is fresh out of the bath. He looks so happy and content. Makes me wonder if I could be that way. And if it can be with Monica.

"I want to but I'm afraid to rock the boat. She's so skittish sometimes."

"I hear ya. Let me talk to her tomorrow and I will get a feel for where her head is at with all this."

"Deal. Can I get her ready for bed? I kinda need to learn if I'm keeping her in a few weeks."

"Works for me. Lizzie is going to be back in a few hours. Gonna go do a few dishes so I'm not left at the altar." Yea right, like Lizzie would do that. They are so much in love it is almost disgusting.

Wouldn't mind Monica and I being like that. Picturing our happily ever after makes me smile. Interesting.

Chapter 11

My father is going to disown me once he figures out what I just did.

"Thank you. Hope your daughter enjoys all of it." I say with a hitch in my voice.

I just sold almost everything I own out of my apartment. Everything. Well, the excess anyway. I kept the necessities and a few luxuries. But only a select few.

"You're really doing this Zandra." Looking around the small room with boxes sitting around filled with the only items I've left to my name. An empty apartment except these five boxes. My life down to five boxes. What have I done? I even sold my Mercedes. That hurt because I just got her at Christmas time.

Buzz. Buzz.

"Yes?" I say through the intercom.

"Monica the taxi is here." My doorman Angelo says.

"Thank you. I will need help with boxes when the moving company comes up. Are they here too?"

"Yes ma'am they just arrived. I will buzz them in."

"Thank you so much Angelo. I will be down when they're done."

The movers took what was left of my life and started for Colvin while I said my tearful goodbyes to Angelo and a few neighbors. I'm not sure I know exactly what I'm doing but it is too late to change my mind now. Colvin or bust.

I get into the taxi for the last time in North Carolina and head for the airport. I will indulge with the jet one last time. I'm sure he will never speak to me again after this. But I know I have to live my own life and forge my own way. And I don't know any other way of doing that. I'm sorry Daddy.

***

"Flowers are dying." That came out worse than I had envisioned. I see Monica flinch at my words immediately making me feel like a jerk. The jerk that I am I guess. I really need to find a way to get over her rejection and be civil.

"I'm sure that makes you happy. What do you want Carter? I don't have time for your crap right now." Oh those eyes are shooting daggers at me. They might even be red like lava.

"I'm sorry that didn't come out like I planned. Forget it." I completely forgot what I even came in the trailer for so I turn around and leave making sure not to slam the door.

"What's it about her that riles me up so much?" I mumble to myself as I walk to the pickup.

"Your ego, that's what." Aaron says from behind me. I jump unaware anyone was around to hear me.

"I know. I'm an idiot. I didn't know anyone was around. You might want to wait a few before going in there. I ticked her off. Again."

"Imagine that." Aaron slaps me on the back but walks in the trailer that has Monica's office in it anyway.

"Brave soul." I chuckle and get in my pickup to head back to the job site. I really am an idiot. No wonder she hates me.

Guess it is time to move on and grow up although, making nice with her and her boyfriend might kill me. But much needed.

***

"He's such a jerk! Thank God I never said yes to go on a date with him!" I slam my desk drawer and yell fully frustrated with Carter and his lack of sensitivity.

"Yes, thank God. I cannot imagine how bad the tension would be then."

Oh snap, I look up to see Aaron standing in the trailer doorway with a king sized smirk on his face.

"Oh, shut up. What is it you want? Are you going to tell me my flowers are dead too?"

"Um, no. You're ticked off because he told you that? I thought it was something serious!" He laughs. Seriously he laughs?

"This is so not funny!" If looks could kill I just murdered my boss!

"Anyway, do you know where Jonathan is right now?"

"I would assume he's at the Piper job site today since the chimney was supposed to go up."

"Okay, I will check there."

"Okay. Can you take these checks to the guys please?"

"Yep. Oh and you might wanna throw these away since they are dead." He snickers and escapes out the door.

"Jerk!" I yell after him knowing through these thin walls he could hear me. What is it with the male species today? Every one of them took their evil pills this morning.

***

Do you think this is funny?

Text from Dad comes through my phone as soon as I turn it back on when we landed at the airport in Tulsa.

Not at all.

"Thank you for the ride. Take care of yourselves. And my Dad. Don't let him get to you." I hug the crew that has worked for my Dad for most of my life.

As I walk towards the terminal at the Tulsa airport I look back one last time. They are all standing and waving. They're like family to me. Family I may never see again.

"Don't cry. Don't cry." I tell myself and continue to the rental counter.

"May I help you Miss?"

"Yes I need to rent a car."

"When will you be returning it?"

"Tomorrow. Do you come and pick them up in Colvin by chance?"

"Yes ma'am. Let me know what time and we will have someone there. You need to make sure the gas tank is full also."

"Great." I sign the paperwork and take the keys to find my rental car trying not to look back to see if the jet is still there or not.

This drive to Colvin really isn't bad. Going to get supplies won't be too tough if I don't order them online. It's helped pass the time thinking about the shop.

Pulling into Colvin, I take a deep breath and survey the new town that's going to be my home. Home. That oddly feels comforting.

I clear my head and pull into the first gas station I see.

"Hello ma'am would you like topped off?" The young gas attendant asks. I nod yes and walk inside needing a cold drink.

"Okay ma'am it will be $37.84 with gas and your drink."

I take out my credit card and hand it to him. He runs it once and scowls. Runs it again and another scowl.

"Is there a problem?" I ask.

"Yes ma'am, I'm sorry but this card has been declined. Twice. Do you have another form of payment?"

I hand him another card but it is also declined. I don't have anything else with me but a large check. The buyer of my life gave me. Daddy must have shut off my cards. He really is mad. What am I supposed to do now?

"Um, let me call my friend that lives here. My credit card company must have shut off my card because of fraud."

"Liz, can you come to the gas station and pay for my fuel? Dad must have shut off my cards."

"Are you being serious? He's never done that before."

"I've never left before either. Please come help me."

"You really came all this way without any money?"

"I have this check from all my stuff that I sold. I never dreamed he would shut off the cards."

"Be right there." We hand up and I look at the poor guy behind the counter.

"She will be right down. I'm so sorry about this."

"Don't be. You're not from around here and they probably thought someone stole your card." If only it were that easy of an explanation. I wish it were that easy. How dumb of me to think Dad wouldn't retaliate? I only sold off everything I owned. Ok, maybe it was everything that he has bought for me.

Could I be any more naïve?

Chapter 12

"Carter? What are you doing clear out here?" I saw when Carter gets out of his car outside the barn I was walking into.

"Tarley I need to talk to you. It cannot wait so I drove here to the 6AB. Do you have a minute?" My goodness he wants to talk to me? This can't be good.

"Sure. Let's go in the barn." I walk into the tack room and hope Carter's following so I don't have to turn around right now. He would see just how uncomfortable I am in this situation. What could he possibly want to talk to me about that would prompt a drive out here?

"Look. I know I've been a total ass to you since I first met you. We all know why but I was completely out of line." Say what?

"Um, you mean Monica I take it?" Is this really happening?

"Yes. I let my bruised ego get the best of me and took it out on you. I'm an idiot who thought he found the woman of his dreams and wouldn't accept her disinterest."

"Wow. Where is this coming from? I have to admit I feel like there are hidden cameras somewhere."

"I get it and I truly am sorry for treating you the way I have. And Monica but that's a whole other apology." Seriously, where are the hidden cameras?

"Why this big change of heart? This seems so sudden. Are you dying or something?"

"Ha, no. I upset her this morning and I honestly didn't mean to. It made me see how dumb and childish I've been since you two started talking, dating, whatever. It was unwarranted and ridiculous. It won't happen again."

"Uh, thank you. I really don't know what to say here." I'm truly at a loss for words.

"You don't have to say anything. I'm gonna go now and lick my wounds in silence. Have a good weekend."

And just like that Carter shocked the day lights out of me and left. Unbelievable.

"I'm telling you there are cameras somewhere." I look down at the barn cat rubbing on my legs. It just meows and moves on with its business.

Crazy day. What's next? A twister? I cannot wait to tell Monica this one.

***

"You're being serious?" I say to Tarley on the phone after he tells me about Carter's visit to the 6AB.

"Very serious. He said he made you mad on accident and it made him realize how dumb he had been about us. Well towards me. About you. My friendship with you." He's stuttering and rambling. How cute.

"He has always thought you were my boyfriend." Now what are you going to say? I'm evil, I know.

"Uh, really?" Safe answer soldier.

"Yep, even though we have only been on one date and it just happened a couple of days ago."

"Yes." He's really struggling with words. Poor guy.

"Do you even want to go on anymore dates with me? Or was it horrible for you?" Hee hee. Ball's in your court now soldier.

"You think you're funny. You know damned good and well that our date was amazing. You're trying to trip me up. And it worked for a minute."

"Guilty. Are you still not going to ask me out again?" Ok tired of waiting.

"I might. But what's this the medieval times? Why can't you ask me?" Good point.

"Touché. Aaron just came in I have to go. Will I see you this weekend?"

"Maybe." He hung up on me with that? He's gonna get a piece of my mind the next time I see him. That backfired completely on me. I was really hoping he was going to ask if he was my boyfriend now. No such luck.

"Why didn't you just ask him out Mon? Aaron says before sitting in a chair in front of my desk.

"I'm not sure." I'm really not sure but I do know I want to go out with him again. That I do know for a fact.

***

"Jonathan, I'm giving you my man card for a bit."

"Why? What happened?"

"I need you to be a girl and ask Monica how she feels about me. I don't know if she wants to move forward or even be my girlfriend."

"Dude, you sound like a girl. You want me to pass her a note asking her to check yes or no?"

"Laugh it up dummy. I'm dead serious here. I'm so far out of my element. And you're more qualified in the mushy department."

"Okay. I will ask. Oh, Lizzie's calling on the other line. Gotta go."

Wonder if she'll answer him. I haven't a clue what this woman wants. Or if I'm even what she wants. She seemed happy with our date but what if she was only being nice? I don't remember things always being this hard with women.

Chapter 13

"Hey Carter, do you have a minute? Jonathan asks when I walk through the door of the Piper site.

"Sure, what's up? Chimney go up ok today?"

"Yea. I need you to do me a big favor." He hands me a $50 bill and smiles that mischievous smile he wears way too often anymore.

"Last I checked you were legal to buy your own booze." Ha. Good one. Sometimes I crack myself up.

"Funny. Lizzie just called and asked if I could run an errand for her but I'm swamped."

"I'm not buying your fiancé tampons and chocolate!"

"You're on a roll aren't you? That's not even close to what I need."

"Then what?" I'm getting impatient and have already had a day worth forgetting.

"Go to the gas station over on the edge of town and pay a bill there. Hurry any chance you can."

"That's it? Going. I'm off till Monday after!" He nods and waves for me to go.

***

I've been standing here waiting for Lizzie for twenty minutes now. The poor kid inside made me move the car up by the building but took the keys as collateral. I'm so horrified and really starting to second-guess my decision to move here.

"Well if it isn't the bronze goddess of my dreams." Oh snap. Not who I want to see me in this predicament.

I turn around slowly trying to plaster a fake smile on my face.

"Carter. Nice to see you. What are you doing here? Getting gas, I assume since this is a gas station?" Wow you're a winner today Zandra.

"Actually Jonathan asked me to come pay a bill for Lizzie. They are both tied up and couldn't do it themselves."

Oh my goodness this just went from bad to so much worse! I'm going to strangle Lizzie the next time I see her!

"Um, I think I'm the bill you're supposed to pay. Well, my gas bill."

"I don't follow." He does look confused. How humiliating!

"Oh my goodness this is humiliating. I got fuel but my credit cards wouldn't work and until I can open a bank account I only have a check made payable to me. So I called my BFF for help and here you are."

"Why don't your cards work?" Oh my...

"My father probably shut them off."

"Uh, why?" Oh for goodness sakes is this man that dense?

"He's mad at me and probably disowned me."

"Same question again. Why?" Grrrr!!!! Do we really have to do this right now?

"I sold all my belongings and came back to Colvin against his wishes." Geez I sound like a spoiled little brat who ran away from home. He has to be thinking that same thing.

"So you moved to Colvin and got cut off by Daddy Rich? That makes no sense." Duh.

"I want to open a bridal salon here but he said no and wouldn't let me have my trust fund so I sold everything I own and am doing it anyway."

"Without his blessing or money." Finally, he's getting it.

"Yes. Can you pay for the gas so I can go hide under a pillow?"

"Are you staying with Lizzie and Jonathan?"

"Oh my goodness! I don't even have a way now to pay for a hotel room!" This couldn't get any worse. Could it?

"They don't have any more room either with Tarley living there. You didn't plan this out very well did you?" A smirk. Seriously? I would like to smack that look right off his face!

"No you jerk!" I really don't need this right now.

"Have you ever not had Daddy's credit card?" Lightning strike me now, please.

"No. I didn't even think about money because I have this check. I'm going to open an account with it and be fine."

"Only one problem."

"What now?" I throw my hands up in the air.

"It's Friday. And it's 6:30 at night."

"So??"

"Bank closes at 5. They wont be open until Monday."

"Oh. My. Goodness! I'm without money, a place to stay and humility for three more days?" Kill me now.

"I got you girl. You can stay with me and I will take you to the bank Monday as soon as they open."

"Stay with you? Are you crazy?" Ok maybe I'm the one who is crazy here because after the day I've had, staying with this hunk of a man sounds like a very good plan. Very bad plan. Who cares?

"I will sleep on the couch. You can have my bed. No big deal. Do you cook?"

"You're serious? You barely know me and know I cannot pay you for the room or food until Monday."

"Do you know how to cook at all?"

"Yes, I actually love to cook. Why?"

"How about you cook for us while you're staying with me and that will make us even." That actually makes sense.

"Deal. But I will take the couch."

"Nah, I couldn't let the princess sleep on my couch. What kind of a man do you take me for?" Oh that smile makes the butterflies start in my stomach.

"I'm not as pampered as you might think. I like camping like everyone else."

"What does camping have to do with this?"

"I mean I can sleep anywhere." That's a different smile. Hmmm.

"Okay, let's get you to my house and we will fight about the sleeping arrangements later."

That smile is going to get me into trouble. Big trouble.

Chapter 14

"You have to get out of your car and walk up to the door Monica. You have to talk to Tarley."

That little pep talk didn't help my nerves any. I drove over here before I knew what I was doing. Subconsciously I knew I couldn't wait for him to ask me out again. I wanted to see him right now.

So I sit here in my car talking to myself in front of his house. Good grief what a loser I've quickly become.

"Just go knock on the door and see him. See that handsome face, sweet lips, strong arms and gorgeous eyes. Oh good grief, get a grip and man up. Woman up. Whatever."

I guess that talk worked because I'm waiting for someone to answer the door. Standing out here like a lovesick teenager showing up at her crush's house without being invited. Wait, lovesick? Nah. Or is it?

"Hi Monica. Let me get Jonathan for you." Lizzie smiles as she opens the door.

"I'm not here to see Jonathan." I totally stuttered through that one.

"Well, come on in and I will go get Arianna."

"Um, I'm here to see Tarley." Duh you idiot she was joking. By the look on her face she clearly thinks you're stupid.

"Jonathan go get Tarley please. He has a visitor."

"He's not here. I thought he went to your house." Johnathan says and walks to us while pushing buttons on his cell phone.

"Oh well, um." Now I'm really at a loss for words.

"Hey man where are you? Oh, well she's here. Ok." Jonathan hangs up his phone with a big smile.

"He's waiting for you at your house. Looks like you both had the same idea." Good grief why is everyone so happy-go-lucky around here? And I'm a bundle of nerves wound so tight they could snap!

"Thanks. Sorry to bother you." I don't look back. I'm so embarrassed! They probably think I'm some floozy that couldn't wait for the man to ask her out. Geez, showing up unannounced what are you turning into?

***

"Thanks Jonathan. I will wait here for her. So do you think this means she wants more than a friendship with me?"

"Why does this woman turn you into such a girl?" He laughs and I have the urge to hang up on him. But he's right, Monica does make me act like a little girl.

"I don't know. You're the one getting married in a couple of weeks not me. This is all very new to me. I don't have a clue how to act."

"For the record, I never acted like a girl when I was trying to figure Lizzie and I out."

"Yea, I remember."

"Hey at least Monica is not engaged to another man!"

"Ah. Okay gotta go act like a girl again. Talk to you tomorrow. Oh and Jonathan…. Thanks for everything."

"Have a good night man."

You would think going up to her after knowing she wanted to see me would be easier than the night of our date but this is worse. The anticipation as we walk towards each other is killing me.

"Hey soldier. Where ya been?" She smiles so that has to be a good sign. Right?

"I went to see this girl."

"Do I know her?" Another smile that makes my heart skip a beat.

"Nah. She's from the big city."

"Tell me about her." I watch as she sits down on a bench right outside her front door. I cannot help but smile when she pats the empty spot next to her.

"Well, she's very head strong. Knows what she wants. Knows who she is. Very intelligent and very beautiful. She kisses like an angel and makes my insides do flips." I take her hand in mine but she wraps my free arm around her shoulders pulling her closer to my side.

I hear her sigh. "You must really like her."

"Very much. I like everything about her."

"Really? Is she your girlfriend?" Wow so there it is. The million-dollar question.

I should have known she would be the one to bring up that subject first. I can feel how stiff her posture got after asking that question and she might be holding her breath. I know my heart is racing.

"Well, you know I'm not sure. We have never talked about where we would go after our friendship. You see, we have only been on one official date."

"Oh wow. So you have no clue how she feels about you? That sounds brutal. Have you told her how you feel?"

"No. I went to her house tonight to do just that."

"What happened?" She shifts her body to where she can look up at me. That face looks so beautiful in this moon light and porch light glow.

"She wasn't there. She must have found someone else to spend time with."

"A strong handsome man like you could take any other man she finds. I don't think anyone could hold a candle to you."

I take that moment to lean down and press my lips to hers. I hear her sigh and relax into me and I wrap both arms around her careful not to break the kiss. Kissing Monica is the best thing I've ever felt. I could spend the rest of my life doing just that.

"Do you want to be exclusive? You know, my girlfriend?"

"Is that wise? That girl you were telling me about will get upset."

"I have a feeling she would be ok with it. Are you my girlfriend or what?"

She leans in and lays quite the kiss on me that leaves me breathless.

"So, I take it that's a yes?" We both chuckle.

"Without a doubt! I would love nothing more than to be your girlfriend."

"You just made my night!"

"I thought you'd never ask!"

"You could have asked me you know."

"And miss your squirming?" She laughs.

"You're naughty sometimes Mon." I pull her close to my side again feeling more than content to have my girlfriend close and happy.

I have a girlfriend, wow.

Chapter15

"You're doing what? Zandra you can stay here."

"Lizzie it's ok. I've made an arrangement with Carter until Monday."

"Zandra you know what I've told you about him and you're already in a fragile state right now."

"Calm down Liz. I'm not fragile. I didn't think this whole plan through and now I have. You're the one that sent him to the gas station anyway. None of this would be happening if you had just come yourself." That ought to shut her up. I don't know how to assure her that this weekend is going to be fine.

"Oh thanks. Arianna was not feeling well and Jonathan said he would go. I'm going to strangle that man. Carter of all people to send to help you?"

"Liz it is fine. Geez I promise it is all good. I need to go though. I'm walking around the grocery store trying to find ingredients for my end of this bargain."

"Ingredients? Bargain? Oh goodness I'm not sure I want to know what you're talking about."

"Seriously Lizzie? I'm talking about breakfast, lunch, and dinner. I'm doing the cooking while staying with Carter this weekend as payment for letting me stay."

"Oh. My mind didn't go in that direction."

"Yes, I know. Now, call me tomorrow and we will talk more then. Bye."

I hang up the phone and shake my head at Lizzie's complete over reaction to this entire plan.

"Did she honestly think we were using sex as a bargaining chip?" I hear from behind me and I'm so startled by the voice I scream and drop everything I had in my arms.

"Darn it Carter, what did you do that for?" I spin around, place my hands on my hips and glare at him.

"I'm sorry I really didn't think it would scare you." He kneels down and picks my grocery items up.

"I don't know anyone here, I had my back to you and you were supposed to be in the car. Sounds like reasons to expect a fight to me."

"I really am sorry. You were taking forever and I remember when I first moved here. This store was so confusing it would take hours to find everything I needed."

"I found everything just fine."

"Peanut butter, salt and tortillas. Sounds yummy. Maybe sex would be a better idea?" Is he serious? Oh my goodness he's the pig everyone has told me about.

"I'm not finished shopping yet. I was going to get a cart when Lizzie called."

"I will help." He grabs a shopping cart and stares at me. Does he really think I'm going to comment on that sex part? Not.

"I think over here are the canned goods. We need corn and a bunch of others." I start towards the aisle when I feel a hand on my lower arm that turns me around.

"I was only joking about the sex. Honestly. I'm not as bad as everyone has probably told you. Well, maybe I was but I'm trying to change that."

"Oh really? And what prompted this sudden change of behavior?" Surely he cannot mean I'm the reason he's changing. Right? That would be crazy Zandra.

"I realized the other day that I've been spiraling out of control and acting like an insane jerk. So I've begun to apologize to those who got the worst of it." How adult of him. I'm intrigued.

"You're referring to Tarley I take it?"

"Geez, Lizzie needs to keep her mouth shut!" He laughs and shakes his head.

"She told me all about that mess long before we knew I was coming here. So tell me, is saving a damsel in distress part of this rehabilitation program of yours?"

"Maybe it is. I think this is going to be fun. Don't you?" Oh. He wants an answer to this one? I would rather answer the sex question.

"Um, the jury's still out." I smile at the disappointed look on his face and start my shopping again. The butterflies in my stomach are going crazy from being in a large store with this man; what's it going to be like in close quarters? Oh boy, maybe I should sleep in the rental car tonight. Oh wait, they came to get that too! I guess I'm stuck with him. I'm not entirely convinced that's a bad thing.

***

"You're freaking yourself out. It is written all over your face. It is three nights and two days. It will give us a chance to get to know each other better and maybe even become friends. Don't worry that pretty little head of yours." She looked like she was turning green and about to run away.

"You're right. I got wrapped up in myself there and Lizzie didn't help matters. It is not like you're a serial killer either. Things will work out fine."

"I only kill the ugly women I have stay with me. You're safe." Whoa, bold move dude. You're going to scare her even more.

"Oh gee, that makes me feel so much better. Let's hope I'm not one of those 'ugly' ones. I better not let you see me without the makeup and bed hair." Oh she has jokes too? Dang maybe this is not a good idea. As she walks away to find more items I cannot help but check her out. She has to be the most beautiful and smart woman I've ever met. This might be the longest weekend of my life.

57

"You know, staring at my backside is not helping me shop any!" Busted!

"Sorry." Not really, but I will say it anyway. From the look on her face she's not convinced. This is going to be the most fun I've had shopping.

Chapter 16

"So, girlfriend, what's on your agenda for this fine Saturday?" I say to Monica over the phone. Sealing the deal on the girlfriend issue last night sure made my load a lot lighter. Not worrying about that frees me up to think about other aspects of where she and I are headed.

"I was thinking of driving to Tulsa for the day and maybe even staying the night."

"And come back tomorrow?" Duh idiot.

"Yes. I would like to get a few things for my house while I'm there."

"Sounds fun." Wonder if she will invite me?

"Wanna join me? Or can you not take time off?" Wild horses couldn't keep me from going with her.

"I can be ready in an hour. Want to pick me up at Jonathan's?"

"Be there in an hour. This is going to be so fun!" You're telling me!

"For sure. I will have you all to myself for two days." Wonder if she's smiling as big as I am?

"And one night!" Holy crap I had not thought of that part. Fun weekend indeed! I think I'm going to love this boyfriend/girlfriend arrangement.

***

"You're going away with him, alone?"

"Oh shut up Aaron! I only stopped by to tell you I was going out of town and to ask if you needed anything from town. Geez."

"I'm only kidding. You two have fun and by fun I mean more than shopping."

"Oh my goodness shut up! See you on Monday." I shake my head and leave Aaron's house.

Before I get the door shut I hear, "Don't do anything I wouldn't do!"

"Unbelievable since that doesn't leave much!"

What's it with men sometimes? Tarley didn't even mention the overnight part but my boss does?

I drive from Aaron's to Jonathan's where I hope Tarley is ready and doesn't make me go inside.

I'm pleasantly surprised to see the front door open and Tarley standing with a suitcase. A suitcase? I would have pictured him as a big duffle bag type since he was in the Army for so long. Hmmm.

"Hello gorgeous could I get a ride?" He says as I get out to say hello. He wraps me up tight in his arms and plants a much-needed kiss on me that leaves me breathless.

"Are you sure you two don't need chaperones?" Jonathan says from the still open doorway breaking us apart and cooling off the moment.

Tarley turns and glares at Jonathan but doesn't say a word. He loads his suitcase into the backseat and turns to me. I'm still standing right next to him not wanting him out of arms reach. Not even 24 hours as his girlfriend and I'm already clingy.

"Want me to drive beautiful? Or do you want to?" Wow he's not insisting that he drives? Nice.

"You can. That way I can look at you all the way there." Cheesy girlfriend now. Good grief, who am I?

"That works. As long as I can hold your hand the whole time." Oh my goodness that smile! Be still my heart.

"Was never an issue. You can hold my hand any time you want." I smile but lean up and kiss his perfect lips one more time before getting in the car.

"I'm really excited about this weekend. Having you all to myself will be amazing."

"I'm excited too. Maybe more about tonight."

"Big plans for tonight? Hope our rooms aren't next to each other so I cannot hear the party all night." That grin again! He knows just how to set the conversation up so I have to broach the big subjects. Pain in the butt already.

"Rooms next to each other? I was hoping you'd stay in mine with me. Is that a problem?" Ha. Ball is in your court handsome.

"I guess if that's what you really want."

Why do I get the slight feeling that he's not so sure about staying in the same room? Surely he's not afraid of me. Did I move too fast and assume too much? Oh great. Way to go Monica.

***

"She wants to stay in the same room? What if I have a nightmare? What will she think of me then?"

"Man it's going to be okay. Maybe you should be talking to Monica about this instead of me."

"We stopped to eat lunch and I excused myself to the restroom. I know she can tell something is off. I don't think we said ten words to each other on the drive here."

"You're hiding out in the bathroom talking to me? Dude, talk to her about it. This is just weird. Beyond weird."

"You think she will understand?"

"Yes you moron. She likes you and wants to spend the night with you. This is Monica we're talking about."

"Geez. You're right. If I want to have what you and Lizzie have then I'm going to have to tell Monica about the nightmares."

"You have not had one for months so it is possible you're over them. Better safe than sorry."

"True."

"She's your girlfriend. Time you let her in. All in Tarley."

"Alright. Thanks for the bathroom chat."

"Anytime. Well, maybe not in the restroom next time."

Jonathan is right. I'm going to have to tell Monica all about the nightmares if I'm ever going to be able to share a bed with her. I sure hope she doesn't run for the hills. What other choice to I have?

Chapter 17

"Poached eggs? Really? Who eats those things?" He slides the plate back towards me.

"Carter just try them. They are amazing, I promise." I slide the plate back in front of him.

"Are you trying to kill me or turn me into an Ivy League hottie?"

"You're so full of it. Just eat the food I made you. That mattress you have is divine and I think I slept better last night than I have in my entire life."

"And I get these as a reward? Dang." That disgusted look on his face makes me laugh. Really laugh.

"I don't think I've ever laughed this much in my life either. It has been fun so far. Thank you."

"So far? What did you expect it to be like?"

"You're just different than I thought."

"Ah. The rumors and what everyone else has told you. Glad I could prove that I really am a good guy."

"One that's ready to grow up, it appears. You have been nothing but good to me. I really hope you realize how much I appreciate everything you have done."

"You're the damsel and I'm the knight in shining armor. Isn't that what you said in the store?" That cocky grin. He's enjoying being my knight too much. But I guess I'm enjoying it too. Damsel or not.

"Yes. If you need any more help being a good guy, let me know. I owe you." And I'm sure these non-PG rated thoughts running through my head are also going through his. Get a grip Zandra.

"I know where to find you. My bed." Holy smokes that grin was electric!

"Alone. But only till Monday." I'm going to leave Monday. Right?

"But we were just getting comfortable."

"Whatever. I'm going to look at apartments today."

"You really don't have to do that."

"And leave you sleeping on your own couch?"

"I don't mind. Take your time finding a place, there's no rush."

"My father would kill me if he saw that I was sleeping in a man's bed I barely know."

"Hey I'm on the couch, not in said bed with you. There is nothing for him to be upset about."

"You're right, but you don't know my dad."

"Not sure I want to if he treats his daughter like this."

"Thank you for saying that."

"Hey, these are not bad." He says finally taking a bite.

"See, I told you. I think you're ready for caviar now."

"Oh my goodness no. And I'm not sure you can buy that in Colvin. Thank the Lord." We both laugh and I start to do the breakfast dishes.

"I will help." He takes the towel off of my shoulder and starts drying the dishes.

"I can't believe you don't have a dishwasher. I though every kitchen had one."

"And you're spoiled. I've never had one and don't want one. I like to get the mess cleaned up and all put away as soon as the meal is over."

"You're a rare breed Carter. It's refreshing."

***

A rare breed? Refreshing? I pray those are both good things.

"So, I need to go by Jonathans today and see about the changes he wants done before he leaves on his honeymoon. After that do you want to go fishing with me?"

"Me? Fishing? No thanks. Besides I have four bridesmaid dresses to finish today so I can get Lizzie's done tomorrow."

"Baby, you would love fishing. Gotta be better than being stuck inside sewing."

"I love it actually. You go catch us some dinner. I will see you when you get home."

"We sound so domesticated. Don't worry I wont kiss you good-bye." I say nervously and we both laugh.

"This does feel oddly real doesn't it? I think we are going to be great friends. Catch some big ones!" She turns and goes to the bedroom. I'm not sure this apartment will ever be the same after she leaves. For some reason that makes me feel a little sad. Hmmm.

"Maysen, you ready to go fishing? I'm stopping by Jonathan's first then I will meet you at the 6AB."

"Alright see you there."

A day fishing with my buddy is just what I need. Male bonding, sunshine, no women and lots of fishing. Sounds therapeutic. So why does my mind keep going back to her?

"Don't get attached man. She's not interested in you like that either. Geez you always pick the unavailable ones don't you?"

Chapter 18

"Carter, come on in. Jonathan is in the back yard with Arianna." She motions for me to go outside.

"Thanks."

"No wonder You're marrying that girl. She has got to be the nicest thing I've ever met."

"That's saying a lot since you have met so many women."

"Ha ha. I'm serious though."

"Thanks. I cannot imagine my life without her in it."

"Puke. What did you want to go over today?"

"I have a little issue that I'm hoping you can help with."

"Okay. What do you need?" This is weird. Why ask me and not his BFF?

"Well, Lizzie and I are going to the mountains in Colorado for our honeymoon."

"The problem?"

"We need someone to go up first and clean the place up. Her grandparents had this cabin all of their lives but no one has been up there in years. Someone keeps it maintained just not clean."

"You want me to fly to Denver, rent a car, and drive five hours to go clean a cabin for your honeymoon? You cannot be serious." He cannot be serious. Why the heck would I want to do that?

"I will pay for everything. I want to make sure it is all set up for Lizzie for our first trip as man and wife."

"Barf. Why would I know anything about that?" He's serious. What the heck is going on?

"I'm going to ask Zandra to go with you but no one can tell Lizzie."

Well, well. We might be onto something here.

"Why the two of us?" I really don't care but I better make him sell me on the idea. He might change his mind if I'm too eager now that I know my new roommate is going.

"She has the woman touch and you have the muscle."

"When I left just now she said she had a lot of sewing to do. You better talk to her before you plan too much." Please say yes, please say yes.

"If you agree then I will call her right now. I will also pay you $1500 to go for me. I know you will miss a few days of work."

"Okay sounds fine. It will be nice to get a little vacation I guess. Even if I'm going to do manual labor." And spend time with Zandra. A beautiful woman all alone with me in the mountains and $1500? Heck yes!

"Okay I will call her. Go get packed and I will book your flights and car. Thanks a lot man. You're doing me a huge favor."

"This place must be a dump if it is going to take several days."

"It has been empty for close to ten years."

"Oh boy. Let me know all the details. You owe me by the way."

"More than you know." Great, how bad is this place? What have I gotten myself into this time?

Can't today. Something came up. Out of town for a few days.

I send a quick text to Maysen knowing he will be just fine without me; I bet Audrey and Abbott are with him.

Cool. We will enjoy without you.

Yep. The whole Correli family is there. Called that one.

***

"Oh, of course! She would love that. Do you have any ideas?"

"Zandra you know the girly side of her better than me so I will trust it all to you guys."

"You guys?"

"Um, I asked Carter to go with you so he could be your heavy lifter. I don't have a clue what this cabin looks like inside"

"Oh wow. I didn't realize he was going with me."

"Is that a problem? I would normally ask Tarley but he's out of town for the weekend with Monica. I don't want to interrupt that."

"Understood. It's no problem at all. I live with the guy so why would it be a problem?" Holy smokes. Now we are going on a trip that spans several days and a remote mountain cabin? Oh brother.

"Do you mind delaying your move until you get back?" Why do I want to say I would delay it indefinitely if he asked? Not appropriate Zandra. Don't even go there.

"Nah, it's all good. I needed to go to the bank first thing so I had some money though."

"I will send my credit card with you so anything you need, use it. Anything at all. I really want this to be extra special for Lizzie."

"We will do it and it will be perfect. Talk to you later, I need to pack."

"Thank you so much! You're the best friend ever to her."

"To you both. Bye now." Okay so what do I pack for a last minute mountain get away?

Chapter 19

"You feeling okay? You were gone an awfully long time. I was beginning to think you crawled out the bathroom window." Thank goodness she smiles after that last part. She cannot honestly think I would run away from her, can she?

"Oh, Jonathan called and I couldn't get him off the phone." Big lie man, big lie.

"Okay. So are you ready to order? I got some chips and salsa with beers to start with."

"You're an angel." I take a big swig of my beer. I need some liquid courage as I've heard it's called.

"Are you sure you're okay? You look pale."

"I need to talk to you about sharing the room tonight." Her smile fades quickly.

"Okay we can get separate ones if it makes you more comfortable. I didn't mean to assume you would be okay with that. I'm sorry." She rattles on without taking a breath.

I reach across the table and clasp her hand in mine which makes her stop rambling. She doesn't look at me though.

"Monica you didn't assume anything. I want to share a bed with you tonight, very much." She looks up at me full of confusion.

"Then what's the problem? You've barely spoken to me since I brought it up back in Colvin."

"And I'm sorry for that. I was so afraid to tell you why but I should have right then."

"What is it Tarley? You're scaring me." Now she's definitely looking at me. Oh boy. Here goes nothing.

"Since I got out of the Army, I've had a lot of psychological issues. I was in the VA hospital in Charlotte for months. The only issue I'm still dealing with is nightmares. While I haven't had any for quite a while, I don't want you to see me like that."

"Oh Tarley. I'm sorry you have to deal with any of that. I'm guessing we're talking about PTSD?"

"Yes, Jonathan came back and had his little girl to focus on but I was alone and let it get the best of me."

"You're not alone any longer. I'm here."

"And that's what I'm afraid will change if I scare you while having a nightmare."

"Not going to happen. Can we eat now?" Wow just like that and she knows it all but wants to eat. She really is my angel.

***

He thought nightmares from being in a war zone overseas were going to make me not want him? If anything, it makes me like him more: a lot more.

"What's that cute little grin about?"

"Well now Tarley, if I told you it wouldn't be a secret. Would it?" We both laugh lightening the mood at last. You could have cut the tension with a knife. His whole demeanor sure has changed too. Poor guy's been stewing over this all day. Heck, probably since we met.

"So, where to first?" He asks and gulps down the rest of his second beer.

"I was thinking the big furniture store over on Magnolia."

"Sure, whatever that is. Didn't you just move here too?"

"I've been here a lot longer than you and have come to Tulsa many times which allowed me to learn where the main stuff is."

"You're pretty smart ya know?" He reaches across the table and squeezes my hand.

"Why thank you. You're pretty bright yourself, soldier." I squeeze back and he smiles. Calm down butterflies, now is not the time.

"Smart enough to snatch you up." Okay now may be a good time for the butterflies.

All I can do is smile and scoot my chair back to stand. I have to get out of this sexually charged situation and get some stuff done.

"Ready? I have a long list to get done today. Then we can relax." I rise up on my tiptoes and kiss his lips lightly and quickly release allowing myself just enough time to walk away before he could grab ahold of me. He touches me now and my list will never get completed.

"Want me to drive handsome? Or you think you can manage?"

"I got it little Miss Independent. Just point me in the right direction."

Chapter 20

Before opening the apartment door, I have to take a deep breath and compose myself. I don't want Zandra to know how excited I am about this trip.

"There you are. We have to leave like ten minutes ago." She's sitting on the couch staring at a pile of suitcases.

"Are you moving to the cabin?" I joke, thankful she laughs.

"Very funny. I don't have a clue what I will need or how long it's going to take. I also needed to take the dresses so I can work on them whenever we aren't busy."

"That sounds reasonable. Let me throw some stuff in a bag and I will carry your pile of them out." I rush towards my bedroom and about fall over backwards when I step inside. It smells like Zandra and there are clothes everywhere. Oh my goodness there are even bras hanging in my bathroom.

"It is like the female twilight zone in here!"

"What's that?" I hear her sweet voice from behind me.

"I said I cannot find my razors in here." Nice save moron.

"They're under the sink in a plastic container. Well, all your stuff is in plastic tubs with labels on them. That way you can find everything when I'm gone."

"You re-organized my bathroom?" What the heck?

"And your kitchen. Hope you don't mind. It is all much more organized now. You will thank me the first time you're trying to find something." She smiles and walks away thankfully before I can have a meltdown.

She has been here less than 24 hours and she has already rearranged my house? Holy smokes. I'm not sure if I'm mad or amused right now. I open all the cabinets and drawers in the bathroom and bust out laughing.

She was not kidding, everything is nice and neat. And even labeled. Wow this woman is a force to be reckoned with.

***

I thought Carter was going to pass out when he saw the changes I made in the bathroom. Maybe I overstepped and went overboard. Nah, he will thank me later.

"Okay Miss Organization, I'm ready. Let's get your bags to the car and get on the road. I already filled up with gas so we are ready to go." I pick up my first two bags and try not to show just how heavy they are. Maybe I over did the packing? He picks up my others and winces too. Okay yes, I did overdo it. Just a little.

"Let's do this. I've never flown into Denver before. Heck I've never been in the mountains either."

"I hope there is a bed for you so you don't have to sleep in a tent."

"What? Why would I have to do that?" No way am I sleeping outside in a tent. Bears could eat me, bugs could bite me and who knows what else. Oh goodness he has to be kidding, maybe I should stay here.

"Calm down Your Highness, I'm only joking. There are several bedrooms to choose from."

"You jerk. I was starting to panic. I've gone camping but in our camper."

"With a shower, toilet and kitchen I assume?"

"Shut up. I know I've lived a pampered life but that's all gone now."

"Whole new woman out on her own for the very first time?"

"Exactly. Except I'm thankful to have you with me so I'm not alone." I hope I'm not blushing even though I can feel myself heating up. Look away idiot.

"So, your apartment hunt got derailed today?"

"So did my trip to the bank on Monday."

"I was serious when I told you there was no hurry finding another place."

"Even after I rearranged your whole house?"

"Yes. I'm sure it needed exactly what you did. Guys really are not good at that cleaning and organizing stuff."

"Oh and that's what their wives are for?"

"Yes exactly. Well not only. That didn't come out right."

"Sexist pig!" I laugh and see he's getting embarrassed. He really didn't mean it that way.

"No, I just meant that men need women to keep them in line and the team they are makes them successful." His face is red now and fumbling over his words.

"Nice save. Do you really believe all that?"

"Actually I do. I've looked at all these new and older couples around me here and they truly are amazing. I never realized what I was missing until Maysen moved here to be with Audrey. Now they are married with a son. It is crazy."

"I've seen a major change in Lizzie too since Jonathan came into the picture. Tanner was a good guy but she never lit up when talking about him."

"That's good because I would say Jonathan is pretty smitten."

"Let's go get their love nest in order. Feels weird to be setting up someone else's romantic night."

"It does. Let's go. We have a long trip ahead of us."

Chapter 21

"You're a shopping machine! We have been to seven stores. Please tell me your list is done; I need to sit down. And eat maybe."

"Um, I believe we have accomplished some that was not on the list. I'm starved too. What sounds good for dinner?" We set all the shopping bags in the trunk and shut it. As soon as I do I wrap my arms around Monica and squeeze. Breathing in her intoxicating aroma is almost too much. Between her hair and perfume my knees go weak.

"Are you smelling my hair weirdo?" I chuckle and feel her also laughing.

"I can't help that you smell so damned good and can't get enough." This time I loosen my hold on her and lean down to press a kiss to her waiting lips.

I could get used to this, without a doubt.

Time slips away from us until her stomach growls so loud the people in the next building could hear. We both laugh and untangle from each other.

"I think we need to feed that animal." Another laugh and quick kiss before getting in the car.

"You know what sounds good?"

"Please don't tell me sushi." I say with a disgusted look on my face.

"Good grief no. Yuck! I was going to say Bar B Que. There's this amazing place that's on the edge of town the way we came in."

"That sounds like Heaven."

"I believe there's a newly built hotel by it too. We can get checked in and walk over to the restaurant. If you want to." If I want to? Stupid question.

"Sounds good to me." I'm still extremely nervous about having a nightmare tonight but it's now or never.

***

I hope Tarley doesn't have any issues tonight. That way he will quit worrying about it. It would sure ease his mind. And mine if I'm honest.

"Hi. We would like a room please. King bed. Nonsmoking." He knows just what he wants. Thankfully it is exactly what I was about to tell them.

"Ok here is your set of keys. You're in room 238. You will find your room has a balcony. Please enjoy your stay. Let us know if we can do anything or if you need anything."

"Wow. He was extra nice. He must have liked you." I tease Tarley as we walk back to the car.

"I have a veteran credit card that always gets extra friendliness when they see the logo. Sometimes I think I should just get a normal one without it but I've had it since our first tour."

"Nothing to be ashamed of. You fought for our freedoms."

"Some people react positive but some think we are asking for handouts."

"If anyone thinks that they need to go see what you saw. I'm so proud of you." I put my arms around his waist and lay my head on his chest. What's this man doing to me?

"You're great for my ego." I feel him kiss the top of my head and put his arms around me. I could get used to this feeling.

***

"That's huge. Sure you can fit?" I tease Monica when we get to the room.

"I'm not sure there will be room for you big guy!"

"I will make room!" I wink at her and see the red tint wash over her face. We have to get to dinner before we're unable to.

"Ready for dinner? The animal is screaming again." She laughs and covers her stomach with both hands.

Seeing her put her hands on her stomach gave me a vision of what it would be like if she were pregnant with my child. I would have thought it would freak me out but honestly it didn't. I'm kind of excited for that day to come.

"Um, Earth to Tarley. Where did you just go?" I snap out of it and look at her. She obviously didn't have the same vision I just did. Probably better that way. She might be the one freaking out if she knew where my mind just went.

"Sorry. Thinking about one of the mares at the ranch." Whoa she would kill you if she knew you were comparing her to a horse. At least it was not a cow. Haha.

"Now you're smiling. What's up with you?" She's clearly confused but amused.

"Let's go eat. I think I'm delusional." I grab her hand and pull her out the door towards the restaurant. I really do need to eat to keep these crazy feelings and thoughts at bay.

***

"Hey, you better answer that." I say to Tarley during dinner when his cell phone keeps ringing. Someone really needs to talk to him. It has rung four times since we've been here.

"I'm sorry. I will go outside and take it. It's Jonathan anyway. Be right back." I watch him walk to the front doors, escape out into the night and soon see him pacing back and forth out front in the parking lot. Must be something exciting by the way he's being so animated with his arms.

Ten minutes later Tarley comes back to the table with a serious look on his face.

"What's wrong? You look like someone just died. No one died did they?"

"Oh no, nothing like that. Let's get back to our trip. Dessert should be here any minute."

"Dessert? We didn't order dessert." Did we?

"I told the server on my way by that I wanted something special sent over."

"That's so sweet, thank you." Be still my heart.

Before I can finish my sentence the server brings over four plates with four different types of dessert.

"Oh my goodness that looks so good!" I might be salivating.

"I was not sure what you did or didn't like so I told them to send one of each."

"But where are yours?" I say and laugh.

"I was hoping we could share." That grin makes me want to forgo the sweets. Whoa girl calm down. Baby steps, baby steps.

"Well if I have to." I say and start with the strawberry cheesecake, then the lemon meringue, then the devil's food and lastly the pecan swirl. Oh my goodness, talk about a sugar high. I enjoyed every moment too.

Chapter 22

"Dang, he even sprung for first class. Will there be a Ferrari at the airport waiting on us?" We both laugh but know at this point it wouldn't surprise either one of us.

"If there is, I'm driving!" I say before Carter can. The pained look on his face makes me laugh again.

"You're not nice." He sticks out his bottom lip like I've seen Arianna do a million times. I smile and shake my head.

"Alright, next stop, Denver." I'm actually very excited about this whole trip. Carter being with me helps but even if he weren't I would still be happy.

"So, tell me about your dad. Why is he so hard on you?" Oh he's going in deep right out of the gate.

"Well, my Mom died in a car wreck when I was a little over two, so I don't remember her. My Dad did nothing but work all the time until I was a teenager; then he remarried for the first time."

"The first time?"

"Oh just wait." I smile and sit back in the seat to get comfortable.

"Oh boy. You're getting comfortable, that must mean it is a long story."

"The first step mom also died but of breast cancer. She was amazing and it was horrible when we lost her. I think that's when Dad decided he wasn't supposed to marry for love anymore and closed his heart off. Even to me."

"Wow. Two wives gone like that, and two moms for you. I'm sorry Zan."

He takes my hand in his and squeezes. He called me Zan. I like that.

"Thank you. It has been tough but Lizzie was always there to help me through. When Dad married wives three through five they only got worse. They were greedy and mean women only after his money and social status. Each one of them found other men who offered them more than Dad could so they would divorce him. He's on number six now and she's younger than I am."

"Holy smokes. No way!" He's shocked to hear that one but that's the same reaction as everyone else.

"Yep. She's twenty-five. First she had a boutique and now he's opening a travel agency for her. Her love of travel will make her great at it he says. He actually expects me to come back to Charlotte and be her secretary."

"Wow. He doesn't know you at all, does he? You would hate being in an office like that." He gets that after barely meeting me but my own father doesn't.

"Guess not. That's why he cut me off. I refused and came here to do what I wanted."

"Beautiful and brave." He squeezes my hand again and I fully expect him to let it go just as quickly but to my surprise, he doesn't.

"Thank you. I don't think my Dad thinks I can make it on my own. He fully expects me to fail and come crawling back to Charlotte."

"And need his money."

"Yep. He knows I've never had to make my own money or even keep track of it. I just did whatever I wanted and he paid the bills; no questions asked."

"Until now. I have to say, I'm pretty much in awe of your dedication and bravery. I couldn't have done what you're doing."

"It's not that big of a deal."

"Actually it is. I had the chance to go in as a partner on Maysen's auto repair shop but I was too scared of it failing and in turn knowing I failed."

"Really? Do you like working on cars better than construction?"

"No. I don't know what I want to be when I grow up."

"Lucky for you, you're just now deciding to grow up." I squeeze his hand we both laugh knowing that's exactly what I'm doing too.

***

She hit the nail right on the head. Growing up is something I know it's time to do. And I'm finally ready to do it.

I'm so blown away by how much Zandra and her dad have been through. No wonder she's the most determined woman I've ever met.

"I don't see how your dad doesn't know without a doubt how successful you and your bridal store are going to be."

She looks at me and smiles the sweetest smile and lays her head on my shoulder.

"I'm really liking this grown up version of Carter. He's good for my self-esteem too."

I lay my head down on hers and before I know it we have landed in Denver.

"Welcome to Denver! It is sunny and 69 degrees today with a breeze out of the west at six miles an hour. Beautiful day for your visit. Have a safe rest of your trip. Thank you for flying with us."

The captain's little speech woke us up from our naps. The flight was not very long but I guess we both needed some beauty sleep. Well, I did but this goddess next to me doesn't need a wink.

"Oh we are here! I'm so excited to get on the road and see where we are going. I remember Lizzie talking about spending some vacations in Colorado but I've never even seen pictures." Her eyes are wide with wonder and excitement. My goodness she's so beautiful.

"Well, let's go then. I've got a Ferrari to drive!" I smile and stand trying

81

to get our bags from the overhead bins in a hurry.

"Yea right. I believe I called first. Cheater." We both smile and start towards the open doors of the plane. Both eager to see what rental car we have awaiting us and where exactly we're staying for the next few days.

"Hi, we have a reservation for Jonathan Doone."

"Ah yes. We have your SUV right this way."

"A brand new Suburban? Seriously?" I say to Zandra when the attendant opens the back hatch of it and awaits us to set our bags inside.

"It's not a Ferrari. I think you can drive this bus. I'll settle for sight-seeing."

"Deal. I bet he got this for any lumber and big things that we might need to get for the cabin. Ready for the next leg of our adventure Zan?" I'm really digging the new nickname I've come up with for her.

"My step mom's the only other person to call me that." She looks sad. Oh great. Did it again.

"I'm sorry, I won't say it again."

"No, it's fine. It's actually nice to hear it again." She smiles and gets in the SUV before I can say another word.

Chapter 23

"Thank you for buying me dinner. This trip of mine has turned into quite the date weekend. You really don't have to pay for everything." She looks up at me and says while we walk hand in hand back towards the hotel.

"I'm a gentleman. Besides I let you pay for all of your shopping today."

"Ha! That you did! So, do you want to go to the hotel bar and have a drink?"

"Yes." How could I say no to that smiling face of hers? I wonder if she's as nervous as I am. It's a good thing she has ahold of my hand because if not she would see me shaking like a leaf. I've never been this nervous about being alone with a girl.

"Could I get a pitcher of beer and two glasses please?" A woman who knows just what she wants and loves beer. They don't make them better than that.

"That's okay with you isn't it?" She looks at me funny.

"Yep."

"You had a weird look on your face after I ordered so I thought I assumed wrong."

"Nope. I was only thinking how they don't make girls any better than you." I lean across the small table and kiss her softly. Whoa maybe I should not have done that. She just ordered a pitcher which means we will be here for a while.

"I just ordered a pitcher. What was I thinking?" Ah, so she was thinking it too?

"My thoughts exactly. Let me go change the order." I stand up and meet the waitress at the bar. Thankfully for us she had not gotten to our order yet. I take the two bottles of beer back to our table and Monica smiles that adorable smile that melts my insides.

"Glad one of us is thinking straight!"

"I'm nervous too don't worry." She scoots her chair over next to mine after I say that. So close I can smell her perfume and hair again.

Not even thinking, I put my arm around the back of her chair and kiss her temple. I hear her sigh and lean into my kiss.

"Now I'm not sure we should even have bottles. Maybe shots would have been enough." She says and we both laugh.

"Or we shouldn't have come in here at all." I pull away from her and grab my beer bottle taking the longest drink from it. For a few reasons because my mouth is dry and I want to leave but won't leave a full beer sitting here.

As I sit the near empty bottle down I see that she has done the same. She gives me a naughty look and stands up.

"Let's go soldier. There are too many people in here." She holds out her hand and I stand before putting mine in hers.

"Lead the way gorgeous!"

***

I don't know where this bold person came from but she's in control tonight! Before I can get the key card in the slot, Tarley turns me around and takes my mouth in his with a passion I'm not sure I've ever felt before. He presses me up against the door and I know I heard him growl a little.

"We probably need to get inside the room before this goes any farther." I whisper once he loosens his grip.

"Get the door open then." Humor even at a time like this. Imagine that.

The second the green light flashes on the door he swings it open and pushes me inside trying to kiss every inch of my lips and neck.

I start to unbutton his shirt and am shocked to see how well designed this

man is. Why am I shocked that a man of his size and military back
ground world be this fit?

"Why did you stop?" He pulls away and looks at me with a worried look
on his face.

"I was in awe of your chest that's all."

"You were enjoying the view then?" More humor? This man...

"Very much. Now take the shirt all the way off."

"No please?" He grins mischievously.

"Not right now, no! I'm too impatient for politeness. Shut up and kiss
me."

Chapter 24

After stopping at the home improvement store we are headed to the cabin. I look over at Carter who is trying to deal with traffic and wonder how I got here. Last week I was coming to Colvin to help Lizzie with her wedding with every intention of going back to Charlotte when I was done and working at that stupid boutique. Now I'm with an amazing man driving through the mountains of Colorado free as a bird.

"You look awfully at peace over there." I turn to see Carter smiling at me.

"So do you. It's really beautiful up here. I'm not sure I've ever seen anything like this before."

"I was just thinking the same thing." He says of course meaning me.

"I meant the trees and stuff out there." I point out the window and know I'm blushing. How can I not?

"It's beautiful out there too. I grew up in a small town outside of Omaha so these kinds of views are not as astounding to me."

"Yes, but Charlotte is the only place I've ever lived and I didn't venture out of the big city. Well, I went to college in New York, which is even more of a metropolis. Yes, we traveled but more like Paris, LA, Hawaii, Cancun, and places like that. I see now why Lizzie wanted to come here for her honeymoon. I honestly thought she had lost her mind when she told me where they were going."

"Not my choice either but I'm sure they will love it."

"I hope we can make it all perfect for them." I really am worried that we cannot get the place perfect enough. Their wedding night is such a big deal.

"I'm sure it will be fine no matter what we do." He doesn't get it; men never do.

"Fine? It cannot be just fine. It has to be perfect and magical. This will be where they spend their first night as husband and wife. This is where they will celebrate the new life they are starting together. I want her to burst into tears when she first steps foot in here."

"Wow. This is pretty important to you isn't it? Alright, you tell me what you envision and I will do my best to get it done."

"You're the best Carter." I smile over at him and feel a bit of emotion bubbling up inside of me.

"Why are you on the verge of tears? Thought you wanted Lizzie to cry?"

"Sorry, I was just thinking that I might never have someone who loves me as much as Jonathan does Lizzie." He reaches over and wipes the lone tear away that slipped out and down my cheek.

"You will. I know without a doubt you will."

"I wish I was as convinced as you. I cannot even get my Dad to love me so how can I hope to find another man who will?" Carter reaches over with his right hand and takes mine in his. It feels so natural to have his big hand wrapped around my little one. The stark contrast between the sizes and skin color is beautiful. Geez. My emotions are running away with me.

"Your father's inability to show you love has no impact on you finding a man who will love you and show you love every day. Because of your dad you will find the one who will love you enough for both himself and your dad." Be still my heart and these tears had better stay away that are burning the backs of my eyelids.

***

I cannot believe Zandra thinks she will never find a man to love her since her dad doesn't show he loves her. If he were here right now I would deck him. How can he treat her this way? She is his only child.

"Tell me why this has you upset." I look over at her and see she's very concerned.

"I've never really told anyone about my life. Sure you want to hear this?"

"I've bored you with my life story. Only fitting for you to do the same. But if you don't want to talk about it, that's okay."

"Oh boy here it goes. Just remember you asked for it." I smile over at her trying to lighten the mood even though I know that once I start telling this story she's going to wish she had never asked.

"Take your time. We have about another hour until we're at the cabin." She squeezes my hand letting me know she means it.

"My parents met in high school. Mom was an outcast because her dad was in prison for killing her mother. Told you it was deep and this is only the beginning. Everyone thought she was weird because she was so messed up but my Dad liked her anyway. His family was one of the wealthy ones in town and never supported their relationship. Mom got pregnant with me after they graduated but she soon got in with the wrong crowd and started drinking and doing drugs right after I was born. My Dad took care of us both but resented us for it. He was not able to go to college like he had planned and his parents disowned him. Things were bad with my Mom going in and out of rehab for my first years of life. Finally, when I was almost nine Dad didn't come home from work on Friday. He never came home again. I've never seen him or talked to him since."

"He just left you with her in that shape?"

"Yep. I don't have a clue where he is or if he's even alive. Mom got worse and had loser after loser around. Sometimes she would go away for days or even weeks at a time."

"How old were you when she started leaving you alone?"

"Ten. I've pretty much been on my own since I was ten. She would leave money on the fridge but it was hardly enough to feed a growing boy for weeks at a time."

"How did you eat? Pay utilities? Rent?"

"She had assistance from the government for all of that I guess. I got a job washing dishes at the diner in town every night so I had at least one meal a day. I saved all of my money to buy a car. Before that I walked everywhere. When I was not in school, doing homework, or sleeping I was working. I moved up to being a cook by the time I was sixteen. By the time I left for college they had decided to shut the diner down but I think they kept it open for me, knowing it was my only source of income."

"Where is your mom now?"

"My second semester of college I got a call saying she and her current loser boyfriend had gotten a bad batch of some new street drug and were dead. Maysen helped me get everything out of that house but it was all so gross we took it all to the dump. Nothing left in that house was worth anything and they tore it down four days later. They condemned it. The neighbors told me that after I left; the house turned into the spot to go for drugs and it was nasty. Even worse than when I was growing up."

"That's where the anger comes from toward my Dad and how he treats me. I wondered why you were getting so worked up about it. Carter I'm so sorry for everything you have been through. It honestly sounds like Hell." She lifts our hands up and kisses the back of mine.

"I'm so pissed at my Dad for leaving me in that kind of a situation and probably have some abandonment issues. It kills me to see your dad hurting you like that."

"I appreciate the protectiveness. It's nothing you need to worry about though."

"I do worry. You're my friend and I really like being around you. I care how you feel."

"Carter. I care about you too but my daddy issues are not something you need to lose sleep over. I'm not and I don't want you to okay?"

"Okay. Oh look I think this is the turn off." She lets go of my hand to sit up straighter and turns toward the door in excitement. But I miss the comfort of her touch probably more than I'd like to admit.

Chapter 25

"So, what do we want to do now? It's only 7:30 on a Saturday night." Tarley asks and looks down at me where I'm nestled in his arms on the bed.

"We could always go see a movie? Or go shopping again? Or go get ice cream?" I say and smile hoping none of that sounds good to him.

"How about we order ice cream from room service and rent a movie on the TV so that we don't have to leave this room?"

"Or this bed." He leans down and kisses my forehead but I was thinking he was going to kiss my lips.

"Don't pout. If I kiss those lips, we won't get room service or a movie ordered. We've got all night."

"We have to sleep at some point." I look up at him and see the panic.

"Yep. Not really looking forward to that part."

"It will be fine. I promise." I sit up and take his face in my hands as I say it.

"I sure hope so." He kisses me then gets up to find the menu book and remote for the TV.

***

I hope Monica is right and the nightmares don't come tonight. If they do I pray she's as accepting as she seems to be and doesn't pack up her stuff and leave me here asleep.

I use the restroom before finding the book where room service and the channel listing is. I look over at Monica and she's put on the white fluffy robe the hotel has for guests and she looks so happy. She smiles at me and actually makes the worries I have ease a bit.

"Quit worrying about me not wanting you after the night mares. It is not going to happen." She walks to me and hands me the other robe.

"You think I'm going to wear this?" I look down at myself only wearing my boxers and back up at her.

"As much as I love this view, I would love it if you would cover up some so I can concentrate on the movie." Oh I get it now. I would probably feel the same way if she were sitting there naked.

"Okay. But don't laugh and don't you dare tell anyone I wore this thing. Especially Jonathan!"

"Cross my heart." She does the invisible X written across her chest. I fake glare at her and she laughs.

"So, ice cream, pie and which movie?"

"I want to watch a shoot 'em up bang, bang movie. If not, I might fall asleep."

"We wouldn't want that. How about a shower while we wait on room service?" I wiggle my eyebrows making her bust up laughing again.

"I could handle a shower. It has been a long day." She walks to the shower untying the robe but just as she's about to drop it she shuts the bathroom door. I walk to it and turn the handle with the forward momentum I have and slam right into the locked door!

"Monica! What the heck?" I yell through the door but all I get back is an evil laugh and the sound of the shower starting. What a pain in the butt! I can't believe she just did that.

"You will pay for this missy!" I laugh at the thought of how easy that was to pull off. I never expected it for sure!

***

"Did you eat all of it? Seriously? I was looking forward to that pie." I step out of the bathroom to find the room service plates are all empty. Then I glance at Tarley and he's looking like the cat who ate the canary. Oh boy this must be payback.

"I was looking forward to that shower too. So I ate all of this to make me feel better." Oh that naughty grin.

"Well played. Are we even now?" I stick out my hand for a truce but he shakes his head no.

"Not even close. You think some pie and ice cream can stack up to the horrible rejection I felt? No way." Oh he's good at this.

"Oh but baby I'm so sorry." I try to put my arms around him but he backs away.

"I'm baby now am I? Well, I think it is time for the movie to start." He pulls up the side chair and sits down.

"You're sitting there to watch it? I thought we were watching it in bed?"

"And I thought we were showering together." Oh my goodness he's so good! Two can play at this game though.

I walk to the bathroom and take off the robe leaving it on the counter. I glance at the mirror and see him watching me.

I take a deep breath and walk out of the bathroom and right by him. I don't stop until I'm by the bed where I pull the sheets back and calmly get under them even though I'm nervous as ever.

I barely get laid down on my side when I hear the TV turn off and Tarley get up from the chair. Before I can even peek, Tarley jumps on the bed and covers me up.

"You're one naughty woman! You don't play fair either!" We both laugh before he presses his lips to mine. Well, I would say we are coming to an agreement of peace now.

Chapter 26

"Oh my goodness, look how beautiful this place is. It's like a scene out of a movie." Zandra squeals and jumps out of the SUV before I can get stopped in front of the cabin.

"It is amazing, yes." That's definitely an understatement. The cabin is right on the river with its own fishing dock, tire swing in the front yard, flowers everywhere, white picket fence, and even a front porch equipped with rocking chairs.

"No wonder this is where Lizzie wants to come for their honeymoon. It is so romantic up here." Her smile hits me right in the chest.

"There has definitely been someone to maintain the place all these years. Nothing outside we have to do." I'm beginning to wonder what in the world we were sent up here for. Unless the inside is falling down around itself we are clearly not needed.

"Can we go inside now? I'm dying to see it!" I look over at Zandra where she looks like a little girl on Christmas morning wanting to see what Santa left her. All I can do is smile and nod my head. Words have completely escaped me. That doesn't happen very often.

We walk up to the front door and just before I slip the key in the lock, I look over at Zandra who is switching her weight from one foot to the other.

"You really are excited aren't you?" I smile at her and receive another huge grin back.

"I'm so excited I could pee my pants!" That makes me bust out laughing.

"Are you sure you don't have to actually pee and that's the reason you cannot stand still?"

"Maybe. Now hurry up please. Or I'm going to do it myself!"

I insert the key in the lock and when it clicks I turn the knob enough to open the door. Before I can get it even an inch she pushes on it and shoves me aside while she walks inside the house.

"Geez, run me over!" I chuckle at the sight of seeing a grown woman wandering all over with her mouth wide open and eyes as big as half dollars.

"This place is so amazing! I expected the stereotypical cabin made out of logs and bulky furnishings but this is more like a beachy farmhouse. It is spectacular!"

"It is pretty homey."

"I could live here."

"Wait. You're telling me the big city girl wants to live in a farmhouse? I thought you would want a high rise apartment with all the sleek and modern touches."

"No. That sounds so cold. And that's exactly how my dad's house is. Now this place is the exact opposite of that! I remember going to my friends' growing up and feeling so much happier in their normal houses. I never let anyone come to mine because it was so depressing."

"Well this house is for sure different. It's getting dark and I bet a fire would be nice." I walk back out the front door in search of a woodpile. Let's hope I can figure out how to start a fire.

***

I'm in such awe of this place. I cannot even imagine what it was like growing up in a house like this. This is exactly the type of space where I would want to raise my own family. I can see myself and two kids sitting by the fireplace playing a board game. All laughing at something their father said who also comes and sits with us. The kids are happy and look just like, what? Carter. My kids are going to look like Carter? Huh? Oh my goodness the man with us also looks exactly like Carter! Holy smokes!

"Have you? Zandra?" I hear Carter's voice somewhere in the distance making me come back to reality. Whoa.

"I'm sorry, have I what?" I can feel the embarrassment start to color my face. Thank goodness he has no clue what I was just envisioning.

"Were you daydreaming about living here or what? You were sure out of it!" He laughs but has no idea the extent of the day dreaming.

"Kind of, yes. Now, what did you ask me?"

"I asked if you knew how to start a fire."

"Not with wood. Dad had the gas fireplaces with the glass pieces. They were more for show than actual warmth."

"Ah. Well, let's look it up so we don't burn the house down before the honeymoon even happens!"

"That would so not be good!"

"We might get disowned."

"Not disowned, more like murdered!" We laugh and start to figure the fire starting process out. I will keep my fingers crossed just in case. Maybe even sending up a prayer would help.

Chapter 27

"Are you ready for sleep yet?" I look down at Monica lying in my arms and see that she's sound asleep.

"I will take that as a yes." I chuckle and lean my head back content with her sleeping so close.

"Ok sleep Tarley. It is time. Things will be fine. Just sleep." I startle at her words.

"I thought you were asleep." Leaning down and kissing her forehead feels so natural. Everything about being with her feels so good. Maybe that will keep the nightmares away.

"I was but could sense your restlessness. Lay here with me and try to relax. Close your eyes and listen to me breathing." She lays her head on my chest and I do as she instructed.

"You're good for me. So good." And I slip off to sleep with only thoughts of Monica.

***

I awoke a few times last night worried about Tarley but he always looked to be sleeping peacefully. He did talk in his sleep quite a bit but if that's all he does during the nightmares I'm not sure what he was so worried about.

I set my hand on his chest and feel his heart beat. I think this man has gotten through all of my defenses and made me fall in love with him. That has to be the explanation for this overwhelming feeling in my chest when I'm near him.

"You smell good even in the morning." I hear Tarley say and when I look up at him that overwhelming feeling grows so big I feel as if I might cry.

"You slept all night. How do you feel?" Raising myself up I smile and kiss his lips.

"You're right, I did." He squeezes me tighter and kisses my forehead again.

"No nightmares at all?"

"I had two actually. Did I not wake you?"

"They must have been mild because every time I would wake up you were asleep and looked peaceful."

"No thrashing or yelling? That's awesome!"

"You were talking in your sleep a little but it wasn't yelling. Is that what normally happens?"

"Yes, when they first started I was in the VA hospital and they had to restrain me sometimes because I would knock things over anywhere near me. I even hurt a night nurse one time. I felt so bad and ashamed."

"Oh Tarley I bet that was terrible for you! I'm so sorry!" I hug him tight and kiss his chest. This poor man has been through Hell.

"But it sounds like they are better."

"Do you still have them every night?"

"I haven't had them very often since coming to Colvin."

"That's awesome. I told you it would be just fine."

"You did miss know-it-all!" Oh that smile again.

***

"I'm going to shower so we can get breakfast." She kisses me and runs to the shower.

I'm so relieved the night went okay. I need to tell Jonathan. I grab my cell phone off the nightstand and see he has already texted asking how it went. He's always one step ahead of me.

Great. 2 nightmares but no issues.

I send and get the thumbs up emoji back. Now I think I might join Monica for that much anticipated shower from last night.

I reach for the handle unsure if it's going to turn or not. It does! I open the door and quickly hear her say, "About time soldier."

"Miss naughty learned her lesson last night I see." I open the shower curtain and get splattered right in the face.

"A little!" She giggles as I look down at myself.

"I'm drenched and there is a puddle the size of Lake Mead in here! The water is supposed to stay behind the curtain you obnoxious woman!" I step in the bathtub and start to tickle her making her scream. A life with her will never be boring. And I want that life with her.

Chapter 28

"Dinner was awesome. Dinner by the fire we built was even better." Carter says while we lounge by the fire both so stuffed we cannot see straight.

"Tomorrow we need to catch some fish for dinner. I bet there's an abundance in the river and would taste so good!"

"Are you going to catch some or just me?"

"Heck yes I will!"

"Have you ever been fishing before?"

"No but I've seen movies where kids know how to do it so it can't be that hard!"

"Are you going to bait your own hook too?" Why is he looking at me with that smirk? Like I can't hook one of those feather things on my line.

"Of course I will. I told you I'm not as pampered as you think."

"We will see about that." That smirk again and one eyebrow raised.

"Yes we will!" I grab the dishes and stomp out of the living room towards the kitchen.

***

She's going to have quite a shock when she has to touch a live worm. I don't know what bait she's expecting but I can almost guarantee it's not a worm. I smile at the thought of her screaming like a little girl tomorrow.

"I don't even want to know what you're smiling about." Zandra looks at me almost scared.

"Probably not." I'm not giving it away now.

"So, I'm beat and think I will turn in. We've got a long day ahead of us tomorrow."

"I will help you make the bed. Which room did you want?"

We start up the stairs but with only two steps made I realize I need to walk beside her and not behind. That view is hard not to look at.

"I was thinking the room second on the right. Which were you thinking?"

"Second on the left actually. Right across the hall from you. Let's get these beds made."

"Beds? You think I'm going to help make yours too?" Whoa she can't be serious.

"Um well I was hoping if we did yours then we could also do mine. But it's no big deal I can make my own."

"Carter, I'm kidding. Of course I will help you. I'm pretty pampered though so I'm not sure I know how to make a bed. My servants did it for me my whole life." She's such a smarty pants.

"Oh very funny. Just help me make this bed please. Leave the sass for after!" I throw a pillow at her causing us to both laugh until our stomachs hurt.

"Seriously though, we did have a house keeper. She made the beds and did the laundry."

"Your life was so rough." I tease her and she sticks her tongue out at me.

"The only thing Dad allowed me to help with was the cooking. And I loved it. There was a time I had contemplated going to culinary school but my love of fashion design got in the way. I enjoyed it more."

"You're the best cook I've ever had the pleasure of being around. If it hadn't have been for that skill, we might've had to resort to bartering for sex!" And this time she hit me with the pillow!

"You're awful. Let's get these beds made before I fall asleep standing up."

"It is so quiet here. You can hear every animal and insect out there." Her head snaps up quickly. I think I said something wrong by the pained look on her face.

"Don't say that. Now I'm going to envision them all coming inside to eat me!" She really is scared. Wish I could tell her I would protect her but that might be going a little too far.

"Sorry. I wasn't trying to scare you. Just meant we can get serenaded to sleep by the crickets and frogs." By the new look on her face I'm guessing that doesn't make her feel any better.

"Eww frogs? Seriously? I don't know what gross stuff is all out there! I don't know if I can sleep now. Thanks a lot you idiot."

"I forgot you're used to traffic, police sirens and all that big city ruckus."

"Colvin was not like that and I slept fine."

"The one and only night and you were exhausted emotionally and physically. I'm glad you slept so well though." In my bed I might add, but I won't say it out loud. But I can't help the pleasant feeling of satisfaction from that statement.

Chapter 29

"I wish we didn't have to go back to reality." Monica says as we near the Colvin city limits.

"I know how you feel. I've got to go help a horse bring her foal into the world so it's not too bad of a reality."

"Awe how sweet! Can I come with you?"

"Of course you can. We can go straight to the 6AB if you want." I squeeze her hand and smile. I cannot wait to include her in every aspect of my life and I'm so thankful she wants to be there.

"Yes please. I don't want to go back to my empty house yet anyway."

"I could come over anytime you would like, you know. I'm just a call away."

"I know but I don't want to be too demanding of your time."

"I would rather be with you than anywhere else." This time she squeezes my hand and we both smile. Maybe reality really will be better.

***

After about fifteen minutes we pull up in front of the barn at the 6AB.

"This is like the maternity ward at the hospitals. Mamas are only brought in here right before giving birth and get to stay for a few weeks after. We like to monitor mom and baby before they are taken outside."

"That sounds smart. Probably easier to spot possible problems from here." I say clearly interested in all Tarley has to say. I feel like a child on their first field trip in elementary school.

"You're catching on quick. This here is Sunshine and she should be ready any minute."

"What do we need to do?" This is so cool! I cannot believe I get to see a baby horse be born!

"We wait around now and when she looks like she's having trouble we will help. Majority of the time they don't need help but you never know. Sunshine is our oldest mare and this will be her last foal. She's too old to start all over and it might impact her health if we tried."

"How many babies has she had?"

"Fiver after this one."

"Wow. She's got a big family like Aaron's." I cannot imagine having five children. That's five pregnancies, five births and five college funds. Holy smokes I'm not sure I will ever have one; let alone five. Yikes.

"Where did you go? Your face turned green and I thought you might pass out." He chuckles.

"I was thinking how having five kids would be insane. Absolutely insane!"

"How many kids do you want to have?"

"None right now!" I yell probably too loud and too quickly. I get a little embarrassed by my outburst and know I'm turning red.

"I know not right now silly. I mean how many do you want? Or maybe none? Just something I would like to know."

"Oh. Well, I've never really thought I'd even get married let alone have children."

"Really? So if I asked you to marry me right now you would say no?" He wants an answer to that? Now?

"Since you came into my life you have changed a lot of things. I'm not sure what I would say. I'd like to know if we're compatible first by simply living together." Oh my goodness I'm so uncomfortable right now I'm not sure I can stand here much longer. Come on horse, have that baby would ya?

"I would love to live with you Monica. After spending this weekend with

you I'm not sure how I'm going to go back to Jonathan's spare room."
Oh boy. Am I crazy for thinking this?

"Why don't you move into my house with me then? We could go to
sleep each night seeing each other and wake up seeing each other too."
Wow so I said it. There's no going back now.

"Are you sure about this?" He can read me too well.

"Yes. I was dreading going home alone too. Heck I'm here watching a
horse's butt instead!" We both laugh alleviating all the tension that had
built up.

Tarley walks up to me and I naturally slip my arms around his waist and
rest my cheek against his chest. I should tell this man that I love him but
what if he doesn't feel the same? I'm so excited for him to move in with
me though. Seeing him whenever I want is going to be so great. And
maybe this will all work out and we will get married and have kids. Who
knows?

***

Well that was easier than I thought it was going to be. I was going to hint
at moving in with her tonight but she did it instead. This woman is going
to keep me on my toes.

"Well, after Sunshine brings Ray of Light into the world and I see they
are okay then I will get my stuff from Jonathan's."

"How much stuff do you have?" She asks nervously. Well, look who has
the upper hand now.

"A few recliners, couches, tables, dishes and bedding. All camo. That
wont be a problem will it?" I look up at her and see she's trying very
hard to come up with a polite answer.

"Um. Um. Y-y-y-yes. We will um figure it out." She won't look at me,
which is probably good because I cannot keep a straight face.

"Monica, I'm kidding. All I have is a bag which I have with me and one box. Nothing big. Mostly clothes. You're safe." I walk over to her and she slugs me in the stomach. I deserved that. But it was funny watching her squirm for a change.

"Not funny. But I probably had it coming." She leans her face up to mine and I cannot help but meet her halfway with a kiss. Hmmm.

Chapter 30

"Well, I'm going to turn in. See you in the morning." Carter says when he stops at my bedroom door on his way back from the bathroom.

"Yes, I will see you tomorrow. If I live through the night." Maybe I should not have told him how worried I am about all the critters outside. I never even thought about us being so far into nature here.

"Zan you will be fine. None of them want in here with us. Just relax and get some rest. I will leave my door open so holler at me if you need me." Oh my that smile is a killer. And I'm being an idiot.

"Oh I will be fine. I just got all wrapped up in my own head but I appreciate you leaving your door open. Good night Carter." I try my best to sound convincing. He must have bought it because he nods and walks to his room. But he did leave the door open so maybe not?

I hear him crawl into bed and soon see the lamp go off. I can hear him thrashing around to get comfortable and I cannot stop my mind from going to a forbidden place.

If only I were under those sheets with him. What would it feel like to have his lips and hands on me? Oh stop it you dummy! You need to sleep! You have a long day ahead of you. Sleep.

***

I awake from a deep sleep to feel someone touching my arm and whispering my name. I open my eyes wondering if I'm dreaming to find Zandra sitting next to me on my bed.

"What is it? Are you okay?"

"I'm fine just totally freaked out. I've been hearing animal howls and I cannot get back to sleep. I'm so sorry to wake you." I can see her smile only a little by the light from the moon. And wow it kicks my heartbeat up to 100.

"It's okay. Why don't you just sleep in here with me? Will that help?"

Sleep with me? Are you nuts Carter?

"You wouldn't mind?" She hesitates before getting up. I can see she's as conflicted about it as I am.

"Of course not. You have never been out here before so it has you a little spooked. It's okay. I wont bite you. We can put the extra throw pillows between us if that will make you feel better." Or make me feel better? That way I cannot touch her sleeping body. I'm not sure I could control myself if I did touch her. And knowing she's so close tonight is going to be torture. But I will endure it if it will make her feel better. Now maybe I will be the one not sleeping the rest of the night.

"Thank you Carter." She constructs the wall of pillows between us and climbs under the covers.

"Goodnight Zan, hope you can rest now." Lord knows I won't be doing any of that.

I hear her roll over and sigh as she tries to fall asleep. When she does I smell her perfume which makes me suck in a quick breath. How am I going to survive sleeping in the same bed as her all night? I'm more attracted to her than I've ever been to another woman. Oh boy this is going to be a long night.

***

I open my eyes and am a bit confused. Where am I? Oh yes I remember. But when I attempt to roll over I'm stopped by something heavy. And hot. And something that groans.

Oh my goodness our pillow wall is gone and I'm wrapped up with Carter. Limbs going every which direction and holding hands! What? Holy smokes what's going on? I don't know how to move myself without waking Carter up. Then the awkwardness will get a lot worse. I'm over on his side of the bed, so it is clear I'm the one who moved the pillows and moved over to snuggle. Oh my goodness lightning strike me now.

"It is no big deal. You got scared and I held you to get you to relax again. We both fell asleep. It is okay." Oh crap he's awake and reading my mind already.

"I'm sorry. I should not have invaded your space. Like it was not enough you had to share half but then I made you share the other half too. I'm so sorry Carter." I scramble out of his arms and out of his bed grabbing my robe and never looking back.

I throw some clothes on and brush my teeth in a rush to get downstairs. I'm thoroughly mortified and the only way I know how to make it up to Carter is to go all out on breakfast. I cannot believe I did that!

***

I don't know what she's so upset about. Nothing happened and I only held her while she fell asleep. Guess I shouldn't have fallen asleep myself, she would have never known if I hadn't.

I take a quick shower to clear my head before going downstairs to breakfast. Zandra will probably eat fast and be out of sight when I get down there. She's so embarrassed and I wish she weren't. I enjoyed every moment of our cuddle session. I probably slept better than I ever have and from the sounds of her breathing she did too.

"Wow this smells amazing." I cannot believe how amazing when I walk into the kitchen. I'm also surprised to find her still there.

"Well, after invading your space completely last night I wanted to make it up to you." She won't look at me as she speaks so I walk over to her and lift her head up by pressing a finger under her chin.

"There is nothing to make up to me Zan. I'm far from complaining. Snuggling with a gorgeous woman all night is hardly a bad thing. Stop apologizing and there is no reason to be embarrassed. We can do it again every night if you would like." I flash my orneriest smile and wiggle my eyebrows. She laughs and smacks my chest.

"Alright enough. Eat so we can get started. We are here on assignment not vacation."

"I would have to say it is both. And don't forget we are going fishing this afternoon."

"I haven't forgotten. You act like it's going to be the grossest thing I've ever done!" This is going to be epic.

Chapter 31

"Tarley that was the most amazing and beautiful thing I've ever seen. Thank you so much for letting me be here for it."

"Well if it's that wonderful for you then I'll call you the next time I have to help. It is not so beautiful being covered in that."

"Eww probably not. This was though. Ray of Light is the cutest and sweetest little thing!"

"He will be with us until his owner is ready for him. We don't let them go until they are almost three months old."

"He wont stay here? How sad. Having to care for them and see them go has to suck." There is that soft heart I know Monica has. She's always trying to be tough but one of these days I will convince her to let down that guard.

"I try not to get attached unless I know they are staying at the 6AB. This little bugger will start a whole new line of champion steer roping horses. His daddy was the best in Oregon which is where Ray of Light will become the next best."

"Awe how sweet. Following in daddy's footsteps. Maybe that's what will make it easier to see him go. Seeing he has a legacy to live up to and carry on in his new home." She smiles no longer looking so sad.

"Very good way to put it. I will be sure to pass that onto some of the guys. They do have issues sometimes letting go."

"Only them?"

"Hey, I've only been doing this a short time. Ray of Light is my first."

"Awe. You guys will always have that unbreakable bond." She bats her eyelashes at me.

"Oh shut up smart mouth. I'm ready to go home now." I emphasize the word home making her face light up.

"Let's go home then." She kisses me before also giving Sunshine a kiss too. Such a softie.

***

"Welcome home." I say as I give Tarley a big hug. I really am excited about him moving in with me.

"Well thank you. This is the first home I've had since enlisting after high school."

"Tarley, seriously? How can that be?"

"I've been in the Army since I graduated high school and when we got out I was in that VA hospital up until I came here." Why does that sound so pathetic?

"Well, I'm proud to have your first home be with me. Please make yourself comfortable." She lifts up and gives me a sweet kiss and all is right with the world.

"I believe that all the Hell I've been through was leading me to you." This time I wrap my arms around her and take that sweet kiss a little deeper. I just cannot get enough of this woman. And I highly doubt I ever do.

"Awe. That's the sweetest thing anyone has ever said to me. Thank you." As she lays her head on my chest I know in this moment it is the right time to tell her how I feel.

"I love you Monica." She raises her head up and looks at me with a shocked expression. Uh oh was that not a sweet thing too?

"Oh Tarley I love you too but I was afraid you were not feeling the same way." Another sweet kiss.

"How about I go show you how much I love you. In our bed." I pick her up and carry her to what's now our bedroom. Love saying "our" everything. Love it so much.

***

"I think I'm going to love having you live here with me. Especially if that happens every time you come home from work!" I smile up at Tarley while we make dinner together.

"I could probably make that request happen." He leans over and kisses me on the nose. That cute little gesture makes me swoon. Such a big guy who has been through Hell but he's still so darn sweet and gentle.

"Deal. I think we are about done here. I'm starved and I love these sandwiches. Who needs a three course meal? Give me turkey, ham, roast beef, mayo and cheese!"

"Don't forget lettuce and tomato. That makes the sandwich." I make a face at him.

"Eww no lettuce please. Tomatoes yes, lettuce no."

"You don't know what you're missing."

"I got sick once from lettuce and have not eaten it since. Not taking my chances again."

"Weirdo. That's probably not even what made you sick."

"Was so." I start to eat making that argument end with a smile.

Chapter 32

"What are you digging holes for?" Zandra is confused and I'm loving every moment.

"You will see. Hand me that bowl please."

"You're so weird. Wait! Oh my goodness what are you putting a worm in that bowl for?" She shrieks when I do it.

"It is bait." She's thoroughly confused now.

"What do you mean it is bait? And why are you still digging?"

"I need to find more."

"Oh my goodness do you mean we are putting those live things on the hooks?"

"Yep." I smile knowing full well she's about to lose it.

"You have got to be kidding me! I'm not touching one of those crawly and slimy things!" She's turning a little green now and I cannot help but laugh.

"You told me you were not as pampered as I thought and could bait your own hook." I raise an eyebrow.

"That was when I thought we were using those pre-made things you buy in the store!"

"Nope. In the wilderness you use worms." I'm loving this a little too much.

"Well you're on your own then. I will work on the house while you go be a wilderness man." She huffs and walks off stomping a little harder with each step.

"Oh come on Zan. I will bait it for you. I was only messing with you." I yell after her but she ignores me. Okay, I pushed her a little too far.

***

I cannot believe he actually expected me to touch one of those things. And to stab it with a hook too? No way. He knew all along how I was going to react. Oh, that's what the look was for every time we talked about fishing.

"That little devil! I will make him pay for that!"

I wait inside until I see Carter's on the dock crouched down probably killing that poor worm. He's oblivious to anything around him so I start towards him as quiet as a mouse. One more step and I'm right behind him and reaching forward to shove him in the water.

Just as I'm pushing on his back he also reaches behind and connects with my wrist also taking me into the river.

"Oh my goodness this water is so cold!" I yell once I come up to the surface.

"You thought you were being sneaky didn't you?" He laughs and shakes his head like a dog.

"How in the world did you know I was coming? I was so quiet!"

"Honey I knew something was coming I heard the screen door squeak and the dock moved a bit when you stepped onto it. So I listened to your footsteps. It was actually luck that I caught your arm."

"Luck? Yuck! I'm in this disgusting water with God only knows what swimming around me!"

***

Wow She's even more disgusted than she was about the worms.

"Watch out for the biting."

"THE WHAT?" She yells completely panicked.

"Some of the fish like to nibble."

Before I can finish the sentence she has started flailing her arms and trying desperately to get out of the river.

"I hate you Carter!" She yells and runs up the bank all the way to the house. I'm laughing so hard the whole time and know she's going to be mad at me for the rest of our trip. But it was so worth it.

I decide it is best to let her cool off and actually try to catch some fish for dinner instead of just scaring them away.

***

After pacing throughout the cabin in fresh clothes I start to calm down. And realize that I honestly don't have anything to be so mad at him for. I was going to push him in so it was only fair I get what was coming to me. It doesn't take long for me to feel bad. He's out there trying to catch our dinner while I'm in there huffing around like a spoiled brat. No wonder he thinks I'm pampered.

I make up a quick batch of fresh lemonade and take two glasses out to the dock.

He looks up and smiles. "Just what I was needing."

I hand him one glass and sit down next to him with my own.

"Thirsty were you?"

"No. I was needing your company. I'm sorry I took that a little too far. I should not have pulled you in with me."

"It's fine. I had it coming."

"You forgive me?" That gorgeous grin.

"Nothing to forgive." I smile back and bump his shoulder.

"Truce?"

"Yes. Have you caught anything yet?" He nods and smiles. This is more like what I had planned for my day.

Chapter 33

"Good morning beautiful." I kiss Monica's forehead and pull her tighter to me. I hear her sigh which makes me smile. I can wake up like this every morning. Almost seems like a dream.

Whoa. Speaking of dreams, I didn't have a nightmare last night. That's awesome!

"Just figuring out you were nightmare free last night?"

"Yes actually. You must be good for me." This time she leans up and kisses my lips.

"I've got to get to work. Hey don't you have to work today?"

"Yes. Told the guys I would be in late this morning."

"Why?" She smiles mischievously and moves even closer.

"So I could enjoy waking up with you in our bed for the first time."

"Awe how sweet."

"Well it's a really big deal to me."

"Me too. Thank you. Now, do you want to join me for a shower?" She wiggles her eyebrows and we both laugh.

"Not going to lock me out this time are you?"

"Not a chance." We race to the shower laughing uncontrollably.

***

I kiss Tarley good-bye and we both head to work. I feel so domesticated and have to admit it feels great. There was a part of me that never thought I would meet a man as wonderful and supportive as Tarley. That happily ever after fairytale might be possible after all.

"Hey welcome back. How was the trip?" Aaron asks when I walk into the office.

I smile and gush, "It was amazing. Got everything I needed and got a little R & R in the process."

"Is that what you kids are calling it these days?" He laughs but I just roll my eyes.

"You're impossible. I don't know how Amie lives with you. The little time I spend with you at work makes me insane."

"Aren't you a funny one today? I see your R & R did you some good. Is the big guy in as good of a mood as you are?" He winks and exits as quickly as he can. Good idea Aaron, I don't want to waste this great mood on idiots today. And we all know he has had more than his fair share of idiot moments. But if it weren't for the biggest idiot moment of his life I wouldn't be here in Colvin and I wouldn't have met Tarley. Okay, Aaron wouldn't have met Amie either but that's beside the point.

"And who might you be deep in thought about?"

I hear Jonathan's voice which brings me back to the present.

"Oh I was talking to myself but thankfully not out loud. What's up?"

"I wanted to let you know that I sent Carter up to Lizzie's family cabin. It's in the Rocky Mountains a few hours from Denver."

"What for? We have a ton of stuff going on and really cannot afford to be shorthanded."

"I know. I talked to Aaron and he said it would be fine for a few days. He and Lizzie's friend Zandra went up to make sure the place will be ready for our honeymoon."

"I see. Well, I hope he can be serious about the task at hand and not get wrapped up in being with a woman alone out in the wilderness. That poor girl has no idea what she's in for." I grimace at the thought of Carter being Carter to that poor girl with no one around to tell him to knock it off.

"She knows what she was getting into. She was living with him before they left."

"She what? Is she stupid?" I shriek probably a little too loud.

"They get along really well actually. And besides he says he's trying to change."

"Tarley's apology is only step one. We will see how long this lasts."

***

"Someone is happy today. Good trip?" A.J. says when he enters the stall I'm in checking on Ray of Light.

"Yes it was great. Always great to get away. But even better to come home. I moved into Monica's house last night." I know I'm smiling like a cat who got the canary.

"Well that's great news. Amelia's going to be so happy to hear that. You were her last couple to match up."

"She can rest easy now. Everyone is coupled up and happy."

"Yes they are. She has sure enjoyed the matchmaking over the years though."

"I've heard the stories. Sounds like a lot of people have her to thank for their happiness."

"Yes but at times they cussed her meddling." He chuckles and shakes his head.

"I can only imagine. What will she do with her time now that everyone is taken care of?"

"Drive me crazy I would imagine." He smiles and walks back out of the barn.

I pray Monica and I can be like them someday. How great would it be to have a family as great as A.J. and Amelia Blake? That sets the bar pretty high but I think we have what it's going to take.

Speaking of Monica, I got a text from her.

Love you.

Awe, I text her back the same. This feels so unreal. But I'm going to enjoy every single moment. If I know anything, it's how quickly circumstances can change.

Chapter 34

"This has got to be the best fish dinner I've ever had. You sure you want a bridal shop and not a restaurant?"

"No. I like to cook meals but one at a time."

"Did you cook for your dad every night?"

"No. When I moved back from New York after college I got my own apartment because I couldn't stand to see him with wife after wife."

"Sounds fair. So you cooked for yourself like this every night?"

"Nope. Mostly take-out. I know that sounds so dumb with how much I enjoy cooking but to be honest it is depressing cooking like this for yourself then eating leftovers for a week."

"Ah. I can see that. You just needed a strong man to help you eat it all."

"I've never been able to find one of those that wanted me and not Daddy's money."

"Did you have a lot try?"

"A few. I've been pretty selective and not easily swayed into getting close to anyone."

"Daddy issues again?" I tease causing her to roll her eyes at me.

"Pot meet kettle." We both laugh.

"Seriously though. Have you always done what your dad has wanted you to do? Until now anyway."

"Sadly yes. I got to choose my college and major, but the rest has been as Dad instructed."

"Are you regretting your decision to break out on your own?"

"To be honest, no. I miss my dad but I don't miss the control he had over me and my every move."

"Are you going to find a place for your shop when we get back?"

"I hope to."

"You don't sound sure. What happened to the Zandra who was going to do what she has always dreamed of?"

"She's scared of doing it alone. Scared of proving dear old dad right."

"You're not alone. You've got Lizzie, Jonathan, Ella Mae, and now me."

***

"I know. I appreciate every single one of you. I'm just afraid I will mess everything up."

"You never know until you try." He reaches across the table and squeezes my hand.

"Very true. I've got to prove to my father that I can do this so maybe he will let me have access to my trust fund early. I really will need more than I currently have to be able to do all the things I've got planned."

"If anyone can do it you can, I have all the faith in the world in you."

"Thanks. Oh, my phone's ringing. Maybe he's had a change of heart already." I run to the other room in search of my phone.

"Hello?" What's dad's attorney calling me for?

"Zandra is that you?" I'm the one you called aren't I? Calm down and put the claws away.

"Yes. What can I do for you?"

"I wanted to call and let you know that your trust fund is not available for you until you're thirty."

"I already knew that. Why are you calling to tell me that?" I'm getting annoyed now.

"Your father said you were trying to access it now to open a store of some kind in Oklahoma."

"Yes. But I only suggested he give me access early but I knew he wouldn't do that. Why is this even an issue? I don't get it."

"I've been going through the stipulations your grandfather had for your trust fund."

"And? Still not understanding why Father is having you research this. We all know I cannot until I'm thirty. End of story."

"Not exactly. I've not talked with your father about this but there is another way for you to get your access."

"Really?"

"Yes but I'm afraid it is a bust also."

"Why is that?"

"Your father can release it to you."

"What? Let me get this straight. I can get my money when I turn thirty or Dad can say yes and let me have the money; whichever comes first?"

"Yes. But since neither of those is happening anytime soon, I'm afraid you're unable to access your trust fund."

"Okay, thank you. Thanks for calling me. Not sure Dad would have told me."

I hang up the phone and stare out the window unaware that Carter is standing next to me.

"Well that's quite the bombshell huh?" I look at him with a questioning look. "Dad says or thirty."

"Oh, yes. Doesn't look like I'm going to get my money for my shop and other ideas for a few years." I sit down on the nearest chair and slump as far as I can without falling out.

"Years? That really isn't fair you know."

"Duh. I know it's not fair but that's how my grandfather wanted it."

"Was he senile at the time?" He laughs and I groan trying to slump farther into the chair, defeated.

Chapter 35

"Well, hello Gorgeous. It's not every day that a woman brings me lunch." I say surprised to see Monica walk into the barn with take-out bags in her hands.

"It's not every day that I have a handsome soldier to bring lunch to. Plus, I wanted to check on Ray of Light." She lifts up and places a quick kiss on my lips. All I do is smile because I really could live the rest of my life like this. She's turning me into a mushy female.

"Ray of Light is perfect but I was needing some food. I've been so busy this morning. Amelia called for lunch an hour ago but I haven't made it in yet."

"I know, she called me."

"Ah. She sent the cavalry huh? Well let's sit and eat then. How has your day been?"

"Just fine. Another day, another dollar."

"I hear ya. Anything exciting happen while you were gone?"

"Actually Jonathan came by today and said he sent Carter and Zandra to the mountains to make sure a cabin is set up for their honeymoon. Poor girl."

"Yea I already knew that."

"Why did you know?"

"When Jonathan kept calling me the other night he was trying to get me to go. But I was with you and I said no."

"Ah makes sense. I cannot even imagine what he's putting that poor girl through."

"Jonathan says he's different with her. We shall see."

"Yep. I've gotta get to a meeting in town. I will see you tonight at home.

I will make dinner." I lean over and kiss her good-bye. Maybe a little too much emotion into that kiss but oh well she can stew over it all day. She smiles and leaves me to ponder my own racing thoughts.

***

"Hey Carter I wanted to check in to see how things were going up there."

"Liar. You're worried about Zandra."

"Okay yes, worried how you're treating her."

"We are just fine. I'm turning over a new leaf. I really like her anyway."

"Whoa. You like, like her? And you're behaving yourself? Who are you and what have you done with the Carter we all know?" We both laugh.

"Funny. I told you I don't want to be that guy. And to be honest I feel things for Zan that I didn't even have for you. Which is weird because I was obsessed with you."

"Yes I remember. Well good luck with her. You're going to need it."

"Thanks. It is really good to see you so happy with Tarley. Honestly."

"Thanks. He moved in with me on Sunday so we are also in uncharted territory. Okay gotta go, just be good to her." Shaking my head at the strange conversation I just had with the man who followed me around like a puppy dog for so long.

And now he's not acting like himself. Hmmm. Could he really be changing for the better? This woman seems to be good for him.

Go Carter!

***

"Yep that's all my stuff. If you need me, you know where to find me." I say to Jonathan when I'm ready to leave his house that night.

"Happy for you man. She's good for you too."

"Yes, no nightmares at all last night."

"I highly doubt you're cured but as long as she knows what she's getting into it will be just fine." He slaps me on the back and smiles.

"Your wedding is next week. Are you getting nervous?"

"No, not nervous but very anxious."

"Understandable. Probably going to be the longest week of your life."

"And that's saying a lot with all the Hell we have seen and been through. Take care man."

"Thanks. You too. Don't forget the last fitting is on Friday for the monkey suits."

"Yep. See ya!" I walk to the pickup feeling excited to be shutting this door and opening the next one where Monica is waiting for me at home.

Our home.

Chapter 36

"I just need to prove to my father that I can do this. I'm an adult not a child."

"Exactly but what do you have in mind?"

"I haven't gotten that far." I smile sheepishly.

"Let's go outside on the porch and look at the stars, drink some beers, and we will figure it all out together." Sounds amazing to me but I feel pretty guilty that Carter has to even think about this mess.

"You don't need to spend your somewhat vacation out here worrying about my problems. I'm sure you would rather be anywhere else." I take the beer he's offering and lead the way to the porch.

"Actually, I would rather be here than anywhere else. I've enjoyed every minute of this trip with you. I care about you and want to help." He sits down in the wicker rocking chair next to mine and smiles that handsome smile.

"You really are an amazing man. I don't care what anyone else says about you. You have been my knight in shining armor since I arrived back in Colvin. Thank you." We clink our glasses like we are toasting and that smile of his makes butterflies take flight inside my stomach.

"Isn't that what friends are for? I know I would do the same thing for Maysen and I'm almost positive he would do the same for me." We both laugh but it doesn't settle the tension growing.

"Friends. I like that. So how do I take what life has thrown me and make the best of it?"

"That's the million-dollar question."

"Twenty-seven-million-dollar question actually." Crap I didn't mean to tell him how much was in my trust fund. I need to quit drinking. Beer acts as a truth serum for me I guess. Good thing I've never been much of a drinker before. Who knows what would have come out of my mouth.

"Holy crap. I didn't realize we were talking that much money. I've got to adjust my scheming then!" He laughs but I'm afraid he has figured out a way to get his own share. Lord knows a hundred others have tried over the years.

***

"I can tell by the terrified look on your face that you're afraid my friendship is going to change like I've won the lottery."

"That obvious?"

"You turned white as a ghost. I don't care about the money Zan. I care about you." Does she believe me though?

"You would think with the way you were raised that you'd want money and the lifestyle that comes along with it."

"It's because of how I was raised that I appreciate everything I've got and I've worked hard for all of it. I don't expect anything that I haven't worked for." I take her hand in mine and see her expression start to change.

"That's so good to hear. I've been duped so many times by men and even women who pretend to be my friend or boyfriend just so they can get access to money or a job with my dad. I've always thought you were different but I got a little scared for a second. I'm sorry I doubted you Carter."

"Hey, dance with me. It is a beautiful clear night and I can use my phone to put on some music." I stand and reach out my hands in hopes she will take them. I want to hold her close right now so badly I'm not sure I will be able to control my emotions.

"I would love to dance with you. You have given me so many firsts since I met you and this will top off the list."

"It has been fun showing you how we normal folk live." I smile and take her in my arms. Oh goodness this feels so right. I hear her sigh so she must be thinking the same thing. At least I hope so. Could I be reading her wrong? I used to be so good at knowing what a girl wanted but with Zan I'm clueless.

"This is nice, thank you. I have to admit I've never really let my heart into a relationship before for the fear of them betraying me for money." She lays her head against my chest and I feel as if my heart is going to beat out of my chest.

"I'm sorry. That's no way to live. Then there's me; the one who never lets himself care too much because everyone always leaves."

"We are so messed up. Two broken puzzle pieces that have never found where they belong."

"Until now." Crap did I say that out loud? I feel her freeze.

***

I cannot believe he just said that. I was thinking those exact words. Could he really feel the same connection that I feel?

"Say something Zan. I can hear your brain working overtime." He loosens his grip on me and looks down into my eyes. From the look on his handsome face I would say he meant every word.

"I don't know what to say since you said exactly what I was thinking." Carter visibly relaxes and smiles. He starts to lean forward and looks at my lips. I cannot keep my eyes from wandering to his.

"Can I kiss you?" He stops right before touching my lips and asks.

"Please." Only word that comes to my mind in this moment. Not sure any others would come if I tried.

The instant Carter's lips touch mine is the best moment of my existence. If I didn't know better, I would think it were July 4th from the fireworks I'm seeing. I've had kisses many times before but never like this.

"Marry me." And the fireworks fizzled out in an instant.

"What?" I step away from him very confused.

"That's the only way your dad is going to see you're an adult and that you don't need his money."

"I'm going to bed. Good night Carter." I run to my room and slam the door shut. What just happened? I knew that moment was too good to be true.

Chapter 37

"Hey Babe, hope you like Chicken Parmesan." I say to Tarley when he gets home. Man, I really love the sound of that. He strides over to me and gives me a tender kiss and watches me finish the salad.

"This place smells Heavenly. And so do you." This time he wraps his arms around me from behind and rests his chin on my shoulder. I could cook like this every day.

"Why don't you go shower and it will all be ready when you're done." He smiles and heads for the shower. I guess now I understand why all of these women in Colvin are dropping like flies into relationships. It really does feel great having someone you love around all the time.

Ten minutes later Tarley enters the kitchen again with wet hair and sweats. Holy crap how do I concentrate on dinner now?

"Um, think you could put a shirt on so I don't drop the food?" I chuckle and am rewarded with a mischievous grin.

"I suppose. You worked so hard on dinner and I would hate to be the reason it was ruined." He pulls a shirt out of somewhere around the corner.

"You did that on purpose!"

"Maybe." As Tarley walks closer to me the butterflies start swarming inside my stomach.

"Are you ready for dinner?" I say breathless in hopes he's going to come closer.

"Yes, but first I want an appetizer." I about fall over from weak knees at that answer. He puts a hand on each side of my face and presses his beautiful lips to mine.

"That will do me until dessert." He says when the kiss is over but I'm still standing here without a voice or thought. He literally took my breath away.

"There is no dessert." I say finally and sit in the chair he has pulled out for me.

"Oh yes there is." He sits and the feeding frenzy begins killing the mood but in the back of our minds we know how this will end.

***

This woman can cook! She's not only smart, funny, beautiful and strong! She's the total package. My total package. Thank you Jesus.

"That was amazing Mon. I'm going to gain fifty pounds if we eat like this all the time."

"Not every night, no. Sometimes I don't get home until after eight. I won't be making a meal that takes an hour to prepare those nights."

"I can cook some too. Grilling is my specialty."

"There is a grill on the back patio that has never been used. It's all yours."

"A grill of my very own? Oh how wonderful." We both laugh.

"There isn't much meat in the freezer but we can go shopping and stock up. We probably need to do that anyway. I barely scraped up all the stuff to make this. I will go tomorrow at lunch."

"I will come to town and go with you."

"Really?" She's giving me a puzzled look? Am I not supposed to go with her?

"Of course. We are in this together. You don't have to do it alone."

"You're going to drive all the way to town to go grocery shopping?"

"Well I have to come pick up some meds and feed anyway. I'll just make it at lunchtime. Maybe we could do lunch at Sally's before?" I cannot wait for everyone to see us together as a couple.

"It's a date. Our first time out in public as a couple instead of friends."

"We are still friends, just a lot more than that now."

"Oh yea?" She says and lifts one eyebrow.

"I don't love Jonathan the way I love you, so I would say you and I are a lot more than friends. You?"

"Of course we are. As far as I'm concerned you're everything to me Tarley. Please don't ever doubt that." She scoots her chair back and climbs on my lap facing me.

"I feel exactly the same way Mon. You're the best thing that has ever happened to me. We better get this mess cleaned up before dessert."

"Nah it can wait. I can't." She wraps her arms around my neck and kisses me with more emotion than I've ever felt. I wrap her up and carry her to the bedroom. My goodness I love this woman.

Chapter 38

Knock. Knock.

"Zandra are you awake?" I say through her bedroom door the next morning.

I got up early hoping to find her in the kitchen like she has been but there is no sign of her.

And now she's not answering me from inside. Well, she had her chance to speak up. I turn the knob relieved that it turns and push it open as slowly as I can. I peek inside and find her room completely empty.

"What the heck?" I check in the bathroom but cannot find her anywhere. She's not in the house at all. Maybe she's on the porch?

Walking out the front door I catch a glimpse of someone sitting on the dock.

"Oh thank Heavens." I rush towards her not exactly sure what I'm going to say. After that bombshell I dropped on her last night she will probably never talk to me again.

Before I get all the way to where she's sitting Zandra turns her head towards me and smiles.

"About time you got up."

"How long have you been out here? I've looked all over the house for you." I sit next to her hoping she doesn't freak out and run away again.

"Since before the sun came up. I watched it rise actually."

"Zan I'm so sorry about last night, I didn't think before I spoke and never meant to freak you out like that."

"Yes." She turns her whole body towards me and takes my hands; smiling the entire time.

"Yes what? You will forgive me?" I'm a bit confused here. What's she saying yes to?

"Yes, I will marry you Carter." She squeezes my hands to reassure me that this was all real.

"Yes? What changed your mind? You don't have to say yes just because. We can go back to the way things were before I opened my big mouth and…." She cuts off my sentence with a kiss. That's one way to shut me up.

***

"Will you let me talk now?" Carter nods his head and smiles.

"Okay so, I've been out here since before the sun came up trying to figure all of this out."

"Did you sleep at all?" Awe he's concerned for my well-being. My heart constricts a little as I look at this handsome man sitting on the dock Indian-style with me.

"No. I couldn't sleep after you somewhat proposed to me. I've never had someone ask me that and actually mean it. While I've been out here everything became crystal clear to me."

"What did exactly?"

"Carter these past few days with you have been the best days of my life. I've felt more alive and frankly more me, than I've ever felt. You and I've both gone through our own personal Hell and are both who we are because of them. I believe that we were set out on the paths we were so we could eventually find each other because like I said before, we are two puzzle pieces that have not been able to fit anywhere until now. I don't care about the money. I just want to continue to be as happy and free as you make me feel."

"Dang that was some speech. Good thing you've been up all night working on it." We both laugh and I kiss Carter when he leans over to me.

"Will you marry me Carter?" I smile at him after the kiss ends. And wow what a kiss that was. I'm surprised I could get the words out.

He smiles and says, "I would like nothing more than to spend every day with you. You have shown me exactly who I'm supposed to be and made me finally see who that is. Thank you."

He helps me up off the dock and engulfs me in his arms as soon as we are standing again. When his eager lips touch mine this time it is like we have never kissed anyone before. Magical and emotional beyond words. How could I have fallen in love with this man in only a few days? Unbelievable.

"I say we get married today." The look of shock on his face makes me a little nervous. Maybe it is too soon?

"How would we do that? We would have to already have a license, preacher, and a witness."

"I called dad's attorney this morning and he has got it all handled."

"This morning? At sunrise?"

"Dad pays him enough to be on call at any hour. He's calling in every favor he can and all we have to do is find someone to marry us and a witness."

***

This woman is a force to be reckoned with. I smile and give her another quick kiss before walking back to the house. Zandra follows behind intrigued by what I'm on a mission to do.

I grab the SUV keys and her hand before walking out the front door.

"Where are we going exactly?" She stops at the bottom of the porch and yanks me back.

"The house down the road is the best place to start. From there we will find out who to contact for an officiant. I don't know where the nearest town with a church even is."

"And then I've got to find a dress. You will need something too."

"Details, details." I smile at her and get into the vehicle. We are getting married today no matter what.

Chapter 39

"Hello Gorgeous. Ready for lunch?" I give Monica a quick kiss and take her hand before walking into Sally's Café.

It seems as if the world stops and everyone watches she and I walk to a table and sit down.

"Well that was weird. You would think no one has ever seen us together before." She says under her breath.

"Yes but never holding hands." I smile and wink at her. I see her relax a bit and settle into her chair.

"Well, well, well. We were beginning to think you two were going to dance around the truth forever." We both laugh and look up at Norma, Sally's sister handing us menus.

"The truth?" Monica says confused. She looks at me but I shrug my shoulders because I'm lost too.

"The way you two felt about each other. We all could tell you were meant for each other."

"It took us a while but we got it. Can we both have the special? Thanks Norma." We hand her our unopened menus and chuckle as she walks off talking to herself.

"I swear, she and Sally live their lives through everyone here." Monica says smiling and shaking her head.

"Who needs a beauty salon to gossip in when there's Sally's Café."

"News about our new status will spread like wildfire now. Hope you're ready and sure about us."

"I'm more than ready." I take her hands in mine across the table and squeeze with reassurance that I still meant what I said.

"How did you know I wanted the French dip?" She says glaring at me. Oops maybe I should have asked.

"Um, we always get that on Tuesdays. Is that not what you wanted?"

"I'm joking. Yes, that's what I wanted. If I didn't want it I would have ordered something else. Good to know you know me so well."

"I know all there is to know about you."

"Probably not ALL but the majority maybe."

***

"Lunch and grocery shopping in one day? How domesticated we are." I laugh that night while readying for bed. Today was great because we did normal couple things.

"Once word got around about us everyone quit staring. I thought old man Jim was going to lose his teeth with his mouth wide open for so long at the store."

"Next time I will do something inappropriate to get them to stop."

"No you wont. You're too much of a good girl."

"You're right I probably wouldn't but I would sure think about it!" We both laugh and get into bed.

"I'm always thinking of doing inappropriate things to you."

"You're such a man! Goodnight Tarley. Love you."

"I love you Monica. Goodnight." We settle in and both quickly drift off to sleep. I pray it is a restful night where he doesn't have any issues.

I spoke too soon. Around 2 a.m. I'm jolted out of my slumber by a heavy arm going over my chest. I open my eyes and see Tarley is crouched down on the bed with his arm across me holding me down. He's yelling obscenities: clearly in the middle of a nightmare. I'm not sure what I'm supposed to do in this situation. Do I wake him or ride it out?

I decide to ride it out and after Tarley has quit screaming he bends down and strokes my face. Just as if he were looking at me I look into his eyes and see tears start to form and fall down his cheeks.

"I'm so sorry. I tried kid I really tried." He's now full on sobbing. It is breaking my heart seeing him completely torn apart inside. What the heck happened here?

Not able to take this any longer I start to rub his hand and saying his name hoping to slowly bring him out of the nightmare.

"Tarley honey? It's Monica. You're here with me now. You're okay. Tarley can you hear me?"

After repeating that and touching his face several times he jolts up and has a confused look on his face.

"What did I do? Are you okay? Did I hurt you?"

"No honey I'm fine. Are you okay?"

He wipes the tears from his face and gets off the bed. When he slumps down on the edge of the bed I see he's ashamed of what he did.

"I'm so sorry Monica. This is exactly what I was so afraid of happening."

"Tarley there is nothing to be ashamed of. You were clearly protecting a child. You were not hurting me but your tears and heart break were awful to see."

"Oh my goodness you were never supposed to see me in that state. This has all been a huge mistake. I've got to get out of here before you get hurt." He stands and gets one of his duffel bags from the closet. As he fills the bag with his clothes I'm sitting here not sure of what to do.

"Tarley please don't go. This is all no big deal. You didn't hurt me."

"I was having a nightmare with you under me, Monica. That's not 'no big deal'." He says with those last words I used in air quotes.

"It isn't to me. I love you Tarley; all of you. I knew what I was getting into from the beginning."

"Well, now I know I cannot be the man you need Monica. I'm broken and I won't allow myself to hurt you during another nightmare." And he walks out the front door. Was this really all a big mistake? My heart doesn't think so.

Chapter 40

The couple down the road gave us everything we were lacking for the wedding. The man is the preacher of a small church even further down the road and his wife will serve as the witness. Dad's attorney somehow got the local sheriff to bring out the marriage license and the couple are donating their own wedding attire. Yes, it is from the 50's but with a little touchup they will be perfect.

"My suit is not going to need much. Are you sure that old dress is what you want to get married in? I'm sure we could find something much more modern in Denver." He looks worried. I put my left hand on his right one that's resting on the console.

"It is absolutely perfect Carter. I promise you these will be better than anything we could ever dream of finding." I'm actually very excited to get them back to the cabin and use the sewing machine that I brought to work on Lizzie's dresses.

"How ironic. We came here to make sure the start of Jonathan and Lizzie's life together was going to be perfect. And now we're going to start our life together first." He lifts my hand up and kisses it. Be still my heart. I cannot wait to say, "I do."

***

We have gotten everything we need and Zandra has been shut in her bedroom for hours working on my suit and her dress. I hear a knock at the door and know it has to be Wilma and George from down the road. She wanted to help Zan get ready and George and I will talk I guess. I had not thought about what we would do while the ladies got my bride ready.

"Come in. She's in the room on the right."

"Well, young man how about we go catch a few fish for dinner? No sense in us staring at each other while those women take hours to get ready."

I love this guy. He's like a grandpa I never had. We talked about a million different things while we fished. He told one about the first time he met Wilma and all kinds of stories since. They have had quite a life together. They kind of remind me a little bit of AJ and Amelia but they aren't quite as old as George and Wilma.

"You know, I met Wilma on a Saturday and by Sunday morning I knew she was the woman I was going to spend the rest of my life with. You and Zandra have nothing to worry about. When you find the one you're meant for it doesn't matter how long you're together. You've got a long life ahead of you."

"Thank you. I pray Zan and I can have a great life like you and Wilma have. You set the bar high." He gives me a big hug and just as we were parting we hear a woman clear her throat. Looking up I'm a little disappointed to see it is Wilma and not Zandra.

"Don't look so upset young man. I'm down to tell you that she's all dressed and ready. Are you?"

"Yes ma'am I am. I cannot wait to make Zan my wife. Thank you for all you have done for us."

"We see ourselves in you two so much. Now go run up and get that suit on."

***

I hear Carter's door open and footsteps go down the stairs. As soon as the front door opens and closes I take a deep breath slowly letting it out.

I am getting married in a few minutes. Wow. Lizzie is going to freak out. Heck everyone in Colvin and even Charlotte are going to freak. I'm not even sure why I'm not freaking out. I just met this man and now we are tying the knot.

Knock. Knock.

I take a deep breath and answer the door knowing it is Wilma coming to get me.

"Are you ready sweet girl? Your groom is outside waiting for you." She smiles and pats my arm.

"I'm. I was just thinking about how weird it is that I'm not freaking out right now. It all feels so right. Oh except we don't have rings. I guess we could deal with that later."

"Actually George and I would like you two to have our wedding rings. We cannot wear them anymore and would be honored if you kids gave them new life."

"Oh Wilma that's amazing are you sure?"

"Very sure. George gave Carter yours and here is the one I put on George's hand 57 years ago. May it bring you and your groom all the love it did for me and George."

"Oh Wilma, thank you so much." I say and look down at the ring I'm going to give Carter in a few minutes. Wow this is really happening.

"Take a deep breath and let it out. Let those nerves go with it. I've seen the way you kids look at each other and like I said before, it reminds me of a young George and I."

"I feel so blessed to have met you and George and for you to be such a big part of our wedding day. I can only pray that Carter and I can be as happy and be together for as long as you two have." We hug and my heart feels so full.

"Let's not keep that young man waiting any longer. If he's anything like George was then he's scared to death you're going to change your mind and run."

"Not a chance. Let's go. I cannot wait to be his wife."

Wilma and I walk down the stairs towards the front door. As we near it I can see Carter standing in the flower garden with George laughing. He looks so dapper and handsome. Happy too.

"That's your soul mate sweet girl." And she walks out to announce that

I'm ready. One last deep breath. Let's do this.

Chapter 41

"He just left? In the middle of the night?" Aaron asks the next morning at the office.

"Yes. I have no clue where he went either. What do I do now Aaron?" I'm at a complete loss here and getting more worried about Tarley with every minute that he doesn't call me.

"Obviously you've called him? Have you called Jonathan?"

"Yes and yes. Jonathan says he hasn't seen him or heard from him either."

"Wow. Thought he would go to his house. What about work? Did you call my parents?"

"Amelia hasn't seen him and said she would call me if she does. I'm so worried about him. He was in a terrible frame of mind when he left." I put my head in my hands and let out a big sigh. My heart is breaking for Tarley.

"I will go out there and look. That's the only other place he can be." Aaron leaves and my heart cannot help but feel a little bit better. If anyone can talk to Tarley about being in a terrible place and coming out of it then it is Aaron.

"Please God let Aaron find him okay."

***

"What are you doing here? No one was supposed to find me until I was ready to face reality."

"Man, I grew up here remember? I used to hide in this hayloft until the chores were done as a kid. This was the only place no one would think to look."

"Did she send you to talk some sense into me?"

"Nope. She's very worried about you. She wants to know if you're alive or not. She loves you Tarley."

"I know. And that love about got her killed last night. You weren't there. It was horrible."

"She told me. It doesn't sound as bad as you're making it out to be. It was just a nightmare, nothing more. You didn't hurt her, only scared yourself."

"I scared her."

"No. You only worried her. Your time in Afghanistan was your own personal Hell and until you're able to share what you went through with her; I'm sorry to say these nightmares are going to keep you away from her."

"Does she want me away from her for good?"

"Man, you know the answer to that. You know her. It is time you two had that talk you're afraid to have."

"I haven't told anyone about that day."

"It is time you did. Maybe then the nightmares will stop. It is worth a try right? She's worth it, don't you think?"

***

Knock. Knock.

I get up from the couch later that evening where I'm trying to watch a movie but keep having to rewind because I'm not fully paying attention. My mind still wanders to Tarley and praying he's okay. Aaron texted earlier today letting me know he found Tarley and he was okay but I still have not heard from him. I'm so worried it is making me sick to my stomach.

"Monica, have you heard from him yet?"

"Jonathan. Come in." I open the door and let him enter.

"Have you? He's not answering my texts or calls. What the heck it going on?"

"I'm not sure actually. He was having that nightmare and when he woke up he freaked out and left. I've not seen or heard from him since."

"That was in the middle of the night. Where the heck did he go?"

"Aaron said he found him and was okay but wouldn't tell me anything else."

"Which nightmare was it?"

"I'm not sure I just know he was crouched over me with an arm across my chest. He kept calling me kid!"

"Oh crap. I didn't know that's what is haunting him."

"What do you mean? Were you there too?"

"Yes, but I didn't see what he saw. He has not talked to you about any of our time in Afghanistan?"

"No. I just know he was in a VA hospital after your last tour ended."

"I cannot really talk about much of this, Tarley needs to be the one."

"And I plan on it." Jonathan and I both startle and turn to where Tarley is standing in the dining room behind us with a defeated expression on his face.

***

"I will let you two talk. Glad to see you're okay man." Jonathan taps my shoulder and leaves the house.

"Are you okay? I've been so worried about you today." The frightened look on Monica's face shoots straight through me. I feel guilty for worrying her.

"I'm sorry, I needed time to myself to process. Time to figure out what my next step is going to be."

"Did you figure that out?"

"I hadn't until Aaron found me. He made me see that these nightmares are my mind trying to come to terms with what I went through. I've never talked to anyone about it and that's probably what's wrong."

"I'm here if you want to tell me or we can find someone for you to talk to."

"I don't want to see a therapist. I want to talk to you. I'm hoping you want me to tell you about my tours."

"Of course I do Tarley. I love you and will always be here for you. Whatever you need."

"I Love you too Monica." I sit next to her on the couch and spill my guts. Let's pray this helps.

***

"Tarley that's absolutely heart breaking. That little boy deserved so much more. You were his hero you know?"

"Some hero. I didn't keep him safe. He died Mon. He died in my arms." I see those tears forming in his eyes and his hands shaking.

"Baby, that little boy was a casualty of war. You kept him hidden for a week. He's the one who came out of hiding. He's the one who made that choice. Not you."

"I know that but I could have done more."

"No, you did all you could. Honey you put your own life on the line while you were trying to find him."

"I should have looked in that car sooner. If I had he wouldn't have been shot. He would have been able to get out of that mess and live a normal life."

"But he didn't. You kept him safe and alive longer than anyone ever had in his life."

"Thank you Mon. It has been like a giant weight has been lifted off of me. I will never forget but I can hopefully move on now." I wrap my arms around him and hold on until the shaking stops.

Chapter 42

My breath stops as Zandra comes into view on the porch. She's literally breathtaking. The lace gown she got from Wilma is perfect just like she said it would be. I cannot believe I get to be with this amazing woman for the rest of my life.

I look down at the ring that George gave me earlier and can't help but smile. This ring was put on Wilma's hand 57 years ago and I pray it will stay on Zandra's even longer. It is the most beautiful setting I've ever seen; unique just like my bride.

"Isn't she beautiful?" I hear George whisper as Zan gets closer to us. All I can do is nod my head for all the words left my brain the second I saw her smiling at me in that dress.

As Zan takes those final steps toward me I get a minor case of the nerves. What if she deserves a man better than me? What if she realizes tomorrow that I'm not worthy of her?

Zandra takes my hand and all of those insecurities fade away. All I see is her gorgeous face and I know in that moment that I'm going to spend the rest of my life trying to be the man she's so deserving of.

"You look gorgeous." I whisper to her and she smiles.

"Today we are here to unite this man and this woman. Today they make the vow to love and cherish each other until death do them part." George motions for me to start saying my vows.

"Zandra I promise to stand by you and love you for the rest of my days. I promise to always be faithful and true."

"Carter I promise to stand by you and love you for the rest of my days. I promise to always be faithful and true."

"Carter as you slip the ring on Zandra's finger do you take her to be your lawfully wedded wife?"

"I do." I slip the ring on her finger and smile up at her.

"Zandra as you slip the ring on Carter's finger do you take him to be your lawfully wedded husband?"

"I do." She smiles at me and puts the ring on my finger.

"By the power vested in me in the state of Colorado, I now pronounce you husband and wife. Carter kiss your bride." I can hear Wilma clapping in the distance as I lift Zandra's lace veil. She smiles at me and once again takes my breath away. This woman is my wife. My wife.

***

Carter puts a hand on each side of my face and presses his lips to mine and I feel as if I've been transported straight to Heaven. Oh my goodness I'm kissing my husband. I'm someone's wife. Unreal.

"Hello Mrs. Greene." He kisses me once more before turning to thank George. Mrs. I'm a Mrs. Ahh!

"Yes, thank you two so much for all you have done for us. You barely met us this morning and look at us all now!" I hug Wilma and lastly George.

"You two gave me the greatest gift and I'm not sure I could ever repay you."

"We never had any children so you two helped us to live out something we always wished we could be a part of."

"Every year on this day you two will be expected back here but to stay with us so we can celebrate the anniversary together!" George gives us each another hug before pulling out the paperwork.

"Let's get down to business and make this official." Carter says and signs on his designated line and I follow also signing.

"You're all mine now, husband."

"I wouldn't want it any other way, wife."

"Alright you two. We are going to leave you to a little quiet celebration but will be back for dinner. We have those fish to cook that we caught earlier."

Wilma and George leave while Carter is giving me another long kiss.

"So what do we do now, husband?"

"I say we make this marriage official." He lifts me up and carries me over the threshold not stopping until we are in his bedroom. It's our bedroom now I guess.

Chapter 43

"No nightmares Tarley. Maybe it helped talking about it. We will just take one day at a time." When Monica leans up and kisses me I'm instantly filled with feelings I'm not sure I've ever felt before. Someone finally knows all my secrets. I feel almost like a new man.

"One day at a time. I love you Mon and I'm so sorry for shutting you out."

"Tarley it is okay. We survived our first fight and worked through it together. Just don't shut me out like that in the future."

"Deal. Want to go to Sally's for breakfast? I'm starving."

"Yes. Let me take a quick shower and I will be ready."

"I've got a better idea. WE will shower and then go get breakfast."

"Deal." That seems to be our new catch phrase. Haha.

***

"I would like the Denver omelet and a side of hash browns. Oh and black coffee please." I hand Sally the menu and smile at Tarley waiting for his order. It will be the same as mine I can almost bet.

"Make that two of what she just ordered." He winks at me and I shake my head but smile.

"Copy cat." I actually love that he orders the same thing I do each time we come in here. I feel that it shows more compatibility between us. I know it's dumb but I like it.

"What can I say? You've got great taste." He raises his eyebrows a few times causing me to bust out laughing.

"That I do. So, how is Ray of Light doing?"

"Good. Walking around and eating all the time."

"Keys to a great life!"

"So, how has it been without your adorning fan around?"

"Carter I take it? It has been the same as when he's here. I ignored him then too."

"When are they coming back? The wedding is this weekend right?"

"Yep. One more couple taking the plunge. Seems like yesterday Aaron and Amie got married. Now they are having a baby."

"It seems Carter, Zandra, you and I are the only ones left."

"Yep. The single table will be all ours." His face gets serious and I'm almost afraid to ask what's wrong.

"Do you think you will ever want to get married?" So that's what the serious look was for.

"If it's to you, then yes. I can see us doing it one day in the future. You?"

"I would marry you today if it wouldn't scare the tar out of you for me to propose." Those eyebrows again.

"Um, wow okay. Never expected that answer." Scare me no, surprise me, yes.

"Want to have kids with me, too?"

"My goodness you're on a roll with these hard hitting questions today aren't you?" Holy crap I think I'm going to hyperventilate.

"Calm down honey, I was asking because I knew that would overload your system."

"You dirty dog! Let me surprise you this time. I would actually like to have a kid with you soldier. Some day."

"Okay I'm the shocked one this time. What changed your mind?"

"I saw the way you were with Ray of Light and to be honest since you moved into my house I can see us having at least one child. Seems natural that we would."

"You realize that we get Arianna for a couple of days starting Sunday right?"

"Trial run, which reminds me I should get the spare bedroom set up for her."

"Hey we don't have to stay at her house now. When he asked I had envisioned us both being there but having her at our house will be so much easier."

"Yes. Man I love hearing you say 'our house.'"

He leans forward and gives me a little kiss before we leave the restaurant and go our separate ways.

Chapter 44

"Good morning Mrs. Greene." I have to say waking up with Zandra in my arms is the best part of the day. This time I know she won't freak out and leave.

"Good morning, Mr. Carpenter." She smiles that devilish grin and when I tickle her she squirms off the bed.

"I don't think so Zandra Greene!" I pull her back in with me.

"Okay I will take your name. How about if I hyphenate it to Zandra Carpenter-Greene?" She's still testing me. This woman is a handful.

"Zandra Greene sounds much better but it's whatever you want honey. It's your name and you'll have it for the rest of your life."

"Really? You don't care if I want to hyphenate?" She's not sure if I'm serious or not. Ha! That's what she gets.

"Nope. You don't have to even change it if you don't want to."

"Now I know you're playing. In all seriousness, I would love to take your name. Part of my new start."

"I'm so glad to hear you say that."

"You would let me not take your name even though we just got married?"

"Zan, I'm not your father. I'm never going to make you do something you don't want to do. I love that you have your own mind. I wouldn't want it any other way." I kiss her one more time and get out of bed.

"Where are you going husband?" She giggles as she says husband.

"I'm going to make you breakfast in bed. Then I've got to get things loaded up so we can go home today. Did you forget we were going home?"

"Yes. I've loved being up here so much I almost forgot this isn't home. I have to finish a little more sewing on Lizzie's dress too. She's going to want to try it on once I'm home."

"Where does she think you are by the way?"

"She thinks I went back to Charlotte to tie up some loose ends with my dad."

"Little does she know you got married before her."

"She's going to kill me for that!" She throws a pillow at me when I'm heading for the door.

"We could always have it annulled." I challenge her.

"Not on your life Mr. Greene. You're stuck with me for the rest of my life."

"Good to know. Be back in a few with breakfast, my lovely wife." Love the sound of that. I have a wife!

***

Almost feels weird to be going back to Colvin. And to be going back married to Carter. Everyone is going to flip out.

"So, do we tell everyone at first or wait until after Jonathan and Lizzie's wedding? I'm not sure how to tell them without Lizzie finding out where we've been." Would it ruin her surprise?

"I will ask Jonathan how he wants her to find out. He's going to kick my butt. You do know that right? He told me to keep my hands off of you."

"You did until after we were married. That says something if you ask me. To be honest, I don't really care about what anyone has to say. It is our life, not anyone else's."

"Very true. How long before your dad finds out? Is he going to murder me?" I laugh but I'm actually most worried about what he's going to say and do when he finds out we are married. I married his only child without his blessing.

"I'm not sure. If I hadn't have had his attorney use connections to get the marriage license he may never find out but...." We both know he's probably going to find out today or sooner.

"Good thing we consummated the marriage last night. You might be a widow by end of day."

"Don't be so dramatic Carter. He's not going to kill you. He's probably going to kill me instead. He's going to be pissed that I didn't make you sign a prenup. I can guarantee you that he will try to persuade you to sign one."

"I will sign whatever you want me to Zan. I told you, I'm not interested in any money."

"I know that. I don't want you to sign a prenup unless it would make you feel better. I don't care what Dad thinks or wants. It is totally up to you. Just be ready because it will happen. I would put money on it."

"Well, are you ready to go back to reality Mrs. Greene?"

"Yep. Ready or not, here we go."

***

"Home sweet home. Well, for now. When I left here on Saturday I never expected to come home with a wife. Now I'm thinking we need to find a house instead of this tiny apartment."

"It's a good apartment. I don't mind living here."

"It's good for a single person. I'm married now so I need to find us a bigger more permanent dwelling."

"Dwelling? Who says that?" She laughs at me and crinkles up her nose.

"Home. Permanent home. How's that? Seriously though. Do you want to find a house or build one? I know this great construction company here in town."

"Let's get through Jonathan and Lizzie's wedding before we cross that bridge. Okay?"

"And dealing with how everyone reacts to the news you mean?"

"Yes." Is she having second thoughts?

"Having second thoughts?" She walks over to me and wraps her arms around my neck and lays the best kiss ever on my lips. Okay no second thoughts.

"Absolutely not. That was the best decision I've ever made."

Chapter 45

"You did what?" Jonathan screams from the other room. Last I knew the guys were having a meeting to go over a new project we picked up while Carter was gone.

"Lizzie is going to kill you. Then she's going to kill me for sending you up there." Oh no that doesn't sound good. I warned Carter not to treat that poor girl like he does most women, apparently he didn't listen. Imagine that.

"Guys, guys keep it down. I'm not sure what's going on but the whole crew can hear you outside. What's going on? What did you do now?" I ask and look at Carter.

"You might as well tell her. I want to see how she reacts then I'm going to know how Lizzie is going to take the news."

"Oh good grief Carter. Did you hurt that poor girl? You couldn't keep your hands off of her either I take it?" This doesn't surprise me but I was hoping he had decided to change like he claimed.

"I married her first." He says smiling and I could do nothing but stare at him.

"Um, I don't think I heard you correctly. I thought you said you married her? What did you really say?"

"We got married yesterday." Oh my goodness I did hear him correctly. What the heck?

"Funny. Why would you joke about something like that? I thought you were turning over a new leaf."

"I'm not joking. We got married at the cabin yesterday." He lifts his left hand up and sure enough there is a gold band on it.

"Oh my goodness. You're serious. You seriously got married? I don't know what to say. Does Lizzie not know?" I look at Jonathan in shock.

"Um, no. She wasn't supposed to know they were there but it's not going to be a secret anymore!" Jonathan yells and paces the floor. Poor guy looks like he's going to have steam shoot out of his ears.

"Carter. What have you done? How did you get this poor girl to agree to this? You just met her." I'm so shocked right not I'm not entirely sure how to feel.

"We really hit it off Monica. You're the one who should understand that. I really care about her and I'm excited about this marriage."

"Care about her and loving her is different."

"I do love her. I can't explain it but I felt like this was what we needed to do. And by God's grace she accepted."

"You found out about the money didn't you? You jerk." Jonathan spits out and I see he's clenching his fists tightly.

"Jonathan, I found out about it yes, but I don't want her money. I told her I would sign a prenup if she wanted me to."

"Wow. Really? Carter maybe you do know what you're doing. Jonathan you need to decide how Lizzie finds out about this before she does from someone around town. How did you get a marriage license without any kind of notice?"

"She called her dad's attorney and he used his connections."

"He's going to murder you. Nice knowing you. You two meet me at the house in thirty minutes and we will see how Liz takes this news." He shakes his head and storms off.

"You sure know how to cause a scene don't you?" I laugh and go back to my desk. I cannot wait to tell Tarley about this.

***

"They got married yesterday? How? Wow." I'm having a hard time believing what Monica is telling me.

"Yes. As soon as they left my office I had to call you. Can you believe Carter of all people is married?"

"No. But he was the one to apologize to us was he not?"

"He says he loves her and just knew he had to marry her right then. It's crazy though because they barely met."

"When you know, you know. I would marry you today. I already told you that." Earlier today to be exact.

"I know but we have known each other what seems like a lifetime compared to those two."

"Are you upset because he's not obsessed with you anymore? Is that why you're so worked up over this?"

"Of course not Tarley. I love you, not Carter. I'm just shocked I guess."

"And a little jealous maybe?" Please say yes.

"Yes. They have their whole lives to figure out now. Maybe I'm jealous. But not that she has Carter's ring on her finger. Good grief. I hope he at least got her a proper ring and didn't just tie a string on her finger." That makes us both laugh.

"We have our whole lives to figure out too. I will propose to you if that will make you feel better. Heck let's go to the courthouse and make it official right this moment."

"No. That's not what I want at all. I want things to happen at our own pace. Not because someone else does something completely insane." Just what I had hoped to hear.

"I couldn't agree more. We moved in together just a few days ago. Had our first big fight and I would like to get a breather before the next big milestone."

"Agreed. See you at home. Love you." She hangs up the phone before I can say it back so I text her instead.

Love you my someday wife to me. Someday.

I'm not surprised to get a quick reply.

Someday you will be my husband. And baby daddy.

This woman cracks me up. I cannot imagine my life without her. Lord please don't let me find out.

Chapter 46

"Hi honey. Hi guys, what are you all doing here? When did you get back from Charlotte? Things go okay? You seem upset." Lizzie says to us and hugs me after Jonathan. Oh boy how is she going to take this news?

"She was not in Charlotte Liz." Jonathan's going to start this off. Okay he can tell her all of it if he wants.

"She told me she was dummy. What are you talking about?"

"I sent Zandra and Carter to Colorado Saturday to get the cabin ready for you. They just got back today."

"Okay but why did you all tell me different? You said you were going home to deal with some last minute details. I'm confused."

"I wanted it to be a surprise when we got to the cabin and it was all set up for us. You weren't supposed to know until we got there." He glared at Carter and I feel like a teenager who missed curfew.

"Okay that's sweet but why are you telling me now then?" Poor girl is completely confused.

"They have something they need to tell you and it cannot wait." Jonathan motions for me to step up and speak.

"Carter and I, um, we wanted you to hear it from us and, um, not someone else." I cannot find the words.

"Is something wrong with the cabin? Did something happen to it? Jonathan do we have to find another place to go on our honeymoon?"

"No Liz nothing like that. Come on guys, tell her." He's clearly annoyed with us and this entire situation.

"Zan and I got married yesterday!" Carter blurts out and Liz and I suck in quick breaths. I'm afraid to look at her.

"Babe are you okay?" Jonathan walks to her hoping to get her to speak.

"I'm fine. Did you two honestly get married at the cabin? Like legally married?" She's a lot calmer than I expected and smiling.

"Yes Liz. I'm sorry if we upstaged your wedding or upset you. That was the last thing we wanted to do." I finally look at her and she's smiling. A big smile. Now I'm the one confused.

"Upset? How could I be upset? My best friend just got married and I'm about to get married too! It is awesome! Yes, I wish I could have been there but I'm so very happy for you two!" She embraces me and tries to add Carter to it. He backs away seeming very uncomfortable. I look at Jonathan and he's standing there with his mouth wide open in shock by the reaction we got. He was expecting Lizzie to throw a fit.

"Oh Liz, I'm so relieved you're not upset with me. I was so afraid to tell you and have it ruin your wedding."

"Please tell me all the details! You two can go back to work now." She shoos the guys and pulls me to the couch. I spill the beans about everything and show her pictures while beaming from excitement and the love I feel.

***

"Well that was strange. You got off easy. I thought she was going to kill you."

"She did take it better than even Zan thought she would."

"You still have Mr. Carpenter to deal with. Pretty sure he's going to murder you. Don't think you're off the hook yet man."

"Gee thanks. But honestly it's okay. I would be happy if he reacted badly because it would show Zandra he does actually love her."

"You do love her. Hmmm."

"Yes. I know I've been a loser for a long time but she makes me want to be a better man for her. And for me."

"Good to hear. Now get to work. No more vacation."

"Right. I might want to have a house built soon. Think we would be able to swing that?"

"I don't know. Aaron picked up another client yesterday. Maybe after that one."

"How long are we talking? Six months?" Ugh longer than I wanted to be in that cramped apartment.

"No, probably be done with the Stark place in about three weeks and could probably start on the new one which will free up the crew on your site for first of next month."

"Wow. Let me talk to Zan tonight and see what she thinks. I just know that apartment is too small for a married couple. Especially not Zan." We both laugh.

"That woman has a personality too big for any apartment. You could always rent a bigger place until you decide what you're going to do."

"True. If you would have told me Thursday of last week I would be married and figuring out a family home, I think I would have laughed for a week."

"Now you know how shocked the rest of us are. You better be in this for the long haul. Liz might have been okay now but if you hurt Zandra she will bury you alive."

"Got it. I won't hurt her intentionally. I'm serious about this. This is not a game to me, I want you all to know that."

"Good to hear. And since we are probably going to be spending a lot more time together outside of work, we might as well get to know each other better and maybe even become friends one day. I'm happy for you two. I cannot believe you of all people got married before me, but anyway!" He smacks me on the back and leaves.

I get inside my pickup and I'm finally able to breathe a sigh of relief. I was so afraid of how that was going to go. Now to wait for Mr. Carpenter to make his thoughts known. Oh boy. Now I'll go tell Maysen. I run by Correli Repair before I go to the job site.

"Hey man. Back from Colorado already?"

"Yep. I have some news."

"Who's pregnant?"

"Oh heck no. Much better news than that. Well in that context."

"What's up then?"

"I got married yesterday at the cabin."

"Lizzie's friend? What's her name again?"

"Zandra Carpenter. Well I guess it's Green now." I can't contain my smile any longer.

"Well, it is about time you got your act together. I cannot wait to meet the new Mrs. Greene. I can't believe you're a married man. Audrey is never going to believe it either."

"Finally, someone I could tell that is happy for me. Telling Jonathan and Lizzie about made me have a heart attack."

"Welcome to the Married Man Club." I smile at that thought. I love it.

Chapter 47

"Guess the singles table is going to be all ours today." Monica says when she comes out of the bedroom. She has been in there for an hour getting ready for the wedding while I've been watching TV in my tux. Women take forever. I simply had to put my tux and shoes on. What is taking her so long to put a dress on?

"Holy smokes!" Those are the only words I could come up with when I caught my first glimpse of her. I've never seen a woman more breathtaking.

"Do I look okay?" She asks even after I was unable to form a full sentence after seeing her.

"You're stunning Mon. Every guy there is going to try and take you home."

"Oh sheesh. I will be the only single woman there waiting for the bouquet toss."

"Ella Mae will be there. And Arianna." I laugh but she just sticks her tongue out at me.

"Funny. There will be no single men there except you so my pickings will be slim."

"So there's a good chance I'll get to take the most beautiful girl home?" I wink at her when she shakes her head at me.

"You're full of it today. We had better get going so you can do your best man duties. You look very dapper in that tux by the way." She wiggles her eyebrows and smiles.

"Glad you like. You really do look amazing." I try to kiss her lips but she shakes her head no and points to the lipstick on them so I settle for her forehead. My second favorite place to kiss her.

***

"Tarley sure cleans up nice Mon." Aaron says and sits down next to me.

I've been sitting here alone waiting for the ceremony to start watching the other chairs quickly fill up.

"Ella Mae loves to host weddings doesn't she?" I give him a weird look. What's he talking about?

"Um I guess so?"

"Oh, I forgot, you weren't here when Karlie and Aiden got hitched."

"They got married here too? I would have thought these two would want something new."

"Oh it's different than Aiden's. This one has a beach theme with the blues and palm trees. Karlie was all about simple and it was actually beautiful."

"How is Amie doing today? Find out Monday what the baby is right?"

"No. We found out yesterday, actually." His grin is making me a little curious but I guess he's not going to tell me.

"Now you decide to be quiet?"

"Sorry, I promised her we could tell everyone together, later at the reception."

"Okay. I will be waiting. Oh here we go. It's go time." I smile at Aaron and feel so much pride when Tarley walks in with Zandra. He is so handsome and so mine.

***

As soon as Zandra and I reach the end of the aisle I cannot help but seek out Monica. Amie, Leah, Karlie and Zandra all look beautiful but I've only got eyes for one woman.

"I'm about to pass out man. It is hot out here and I cannot breathe with this dumb bowtie on." Jonathan whispers to me right before the pastor joins us.

"Breathe Jonathan. You're just nervous. Lizzie is the love of your life and she will be down here in a minute. Calm down before you pass out and ruin her day." Just as I finish my speech the wedding march starts playing and we see Lizzie emerge from the house.

I hear Jonathan suck in a quick breath as he sees his future wife for the first time in her wedding gown. She smiles at him and I feel his body relax. Yep, just needed her. That's when I look at Monica again and know without a doubt she's the one I'm going to marry. When she smiles at me my heart does a flip inside my chest and I smile back. Man, I love that beautiful woman.

"Thank you all for joining us today to unite Jonathan and Lizzie in holy matrimony. I've had the joy of uniting the majority of you here and I'm proud to be asked again."

"Jonathan Doone, do you take Elizabeth Kentis to be your wife until death do you part?"

"I most certainly do."

"Elizabeth Kentis, do you take Jonathan Doone to be your husband until death do you part?"

"Yes I do." I look over at Monica again to find she's wiping tears away. Hmmm. There's that soft side again.

"Lizzie I give you this ring for you to wear but more importantly I want you to always have it as a symbol of how much I love you. Forever."

"Jonathan I give you this ring as a token of the love I feel inside for you but so that the world will always know that you're mine. Forever."

"Jonathan you may kiss your bride."

"I would like to introduce to you for the first time as a married couple, Jonathan and Lizzie Doone."

Everyone stands and claps so Jonathan steals another kiss from his wife. My attention slips to Zandra who smiles and blows a kiss to Carter. Her husband. Good grief everyone is married except me and Monica. Maybe I should do something about that. She would probably kill me though.

"You're next." I turn my head to look at Zandra as we follow the happy couple down the aisle.

"Oh you think so do you?"

"I've seen you two together. It's obvious you two love each other and have found the one. What's stopping you?"

"Nothing now. Congrats on your wedding." I pat her hand and go off in search of my girl.

"Hey handsome. Who you looking for?" Ah, there she is.

"There is this amazing woman that I'm so in love with. Have you seen her?" I take her in my arms and she finally lets me kiss her. And what a kiss it is!

Chapter 48

"Do you regret not having a wedding like this?" Carter says into my ear while we slow dance at the reception.

"Not at all. I loved our wedding. It was perfect." I give him a smile and sweet kiss of reassurance.

"I agree. This all seems like such a production but ours was all about us and our vows." I love this man but I'm afraid he only married me out of obligation, or pity. Probably more likely to be out of pity.

"It was a beautiful production though."

"That it was. It is about time for your speech. Are you ready? I know Tarley is."

"Speech? No one said I had to make a speech." I glare.

"Maid of Honor and Best Man always make speeches or toasts rather at the reception."

"Oh snap. I never even thought of that. Dang! I'll go with whatever pops into my head."

"Lord help us! Just kidding. Say exactly how you feel when you look at Jonathan and Lizzie."

"You wanna make it for me? You seem to have it all worked out already." I tease and he turns green.

"Absolutely not. I don't like speaking in public."

"You're no help then." We break apart as the song ends and make our way back to the table.

***

Once everyone is back in their seats we are expecting the best man to start with his speech but instead Lizzie stands up with her glass in hand.

"I know you're all expecting the speeches but Jonathan and I wanted to take a moment to ask you all to raise up your glasses for another special couple. My best friend Zandra got married herself a few days ago. While we all know Carter as the wild child that came to town with Maysen Correli, we are so pleased that he and Zandra found each other here in Colvin. We love you guys and wish you all the love and happiness!"

I look over at Zandra and clink her glass with mine. I expected her to be beyond embarrassed but instead she's almost sad. I wipe away one of the tears that ran down her cheek and she smiles.

"What's wrong? Please tell me those are happy tears."

"They are. I'm so touched that they took time out of their own celebration to do that. Amazing people. It is truly an amazing community." More tears my goodness.

"Don't cry. Your speech is next and I would hate for your makeup to be messed up. You would hate those pictures forever." I wink at her and smile.

"You're so right." She wipes the tears away and takes a deep breath.

"Here is to us Zan. May we have as much happiness as the other couples here in Colvin."

I lean over and give her a quick kiss on the lips. I'm beyond thankful for this woman.

***

Clink. Clink. Clink.

I tap my glass with a fork trying to get everyone's attention. Once I do I feel the panic start to creep up with all those eyes all being on me. Oh boy.

"If I could have your attention please. Thank you. I met Elizabeth Kentis Doone when we were children both living in Charlotte. She was always the artsy friend who could paint a picture just from memory, while I was the one who couldn't draw a stick figure. Liz had tragedy strike in her life too many times for one person. Liz, your mom and Marianna are looking down right now so proud of you and so incredibly happy you found Jonathan. He came along and made your and Arianna's life complete. When I look at how much in love you two are it makes me believe in fairytales and happily-ever-afters. May you always be as happy and in love as you are in this moment. Love you both, congratulations."

I sit down and breathe a sigh of relief as everyone clinks their glasses.

"Oh thank goodness that's over!" I lean against Carter's shoulder and relax.

"That was beautiful Zan. You're good at 'whatever comes to mind'. A lot better than I thought. You rocked it."

"Thank you. After her speech to us I had to make it special. Now could we go dance again? I love this song. And wouldn't mind being in your arms again." I smile and let him lead me back on to the dance floor. This week has been amazing and I couldn't be happier.

Chapter 49

"As I'm sure all of you know, Jonathan and I served in the Army together for what seemed like forever. He always had my back and I had his. Until he met Lizzie. Then it was all about her. Haha just joking. He and I went through Hell together and as soon as he met the love of his life he was healed. He no longer worried about the past; only looked forward to being with Lizzie and Arianna. I could sure tell you some wild stories but the best is yet to come for these two. The future looks bright and so much love and happiness awaits in your next adventure. You couldn't have chosen a more loyal and honest man Lizzie. He's the best there is and I wish you three the best. Love you guys."

"I think you're the best man out there." Monica whispers in my ear after I take my seat again.

"I'm so glad that's over with. I hate speaking like that in front of so many people."

"You did a great job. I think Jonathan even teared up a little." She gives me a kiss on the lips making my heart swell with pride. This is the woman I want to spend the rest of my live with. No doubt.

"Wanna dance beautiful? I could really use some alone time without anyone looking at me." I lead her to a dark corner on the dance floor and hold her close. As close as I can possibly get her.

***

Clink. Clink. Clink

"Could we get your attention one more time? We've got something we would like to say while everyone is gathered in one place. Amie and I are expecting as you all know but we went to our ultrasound appointment the yesterday and found out the sex. We'd like to share that news with those most important in our lives. Thankfully all of you are right here."

Everyone cheers and when the crowd quiets down Aaron continues while Amie stands beside him with a huge grin on her face.

"Well, we are having a little girl." Everyone cheers again.

"And a boy." Everyone gets completely silent this time.

"Yes. We are having twins!" The whole place erupts in cheers and happiness for Aaron and Amie. One by one they're met with hugs and well wishes. All the while beaming from ear to ear.

***

Dancing here in Tarley's arms makes me so excited about our future. Two couples in one week getting hitched is almost too much to handle. Fairytale overload but I cannot help but hope that someday it will be me and Tarley getting the toasts. He's so darned hot in that tux how could I not?

"You're smiling. Watcha thinking about?" He kisses my forehead making me sigh.

"Just how happy I am for both new couples. And that it might be us one day." I look up at him in hopes to read his thoughts to that admission on his face. No such luck. He pulls me tighter like he's changing the subject.

"It will be." After a few long and silent moments he finally answers.

"That was a long pause before you answered. Having second thoughts about us?" Please say no. Please say no.

"Not on your life." Whew.

"Then why the hesitation?" I'm getting a bit upset at his lack of emotion. Could he be having second thoughts? Of course he would now that I'm all in and actually thinking about marriage and kids.

"I was trying to decide if Jonathan would kill me or not if I dropped to one knee right now." Holy crap.

"Oh my goodness Tarley you cannot be serious."

"You're so confusing, you know that? One minute you're ticked that I don't jump on the wedding bandwagon then when I do you jump off.

178

I've got whip lash Mon."

"You're right. I'm confusing myself. I'm a mess." I storm off to find somewhere Tarley isn't. I've got to get my head on straight before I blow this whole thing!

***

"Well buddy, it's your turn. Are you two ready?"

"Not even close. So, your mom is bringing Arianna over in the morning before she leaves, right?"

"Yep. She said about nine. She will be back Monday afternoon now instead of Wednesday."

"She doesn't think we can handle her?" She's probably right but he doesn't need to know that.

"No. Karlie is staying and Mom needs to get back for the shop anyway."

"Uh huh. Anyway, you two have a great honeymoon. We have got it under control here. Congrats." I slap him on the back and go in search of Monica.

"Hey love. We better go get some rest before the tornado shows up at nine tomorrow morning." I smile and so does she, but her smile doesn't reach her eyes.

"I'm sorry Tarley. I love you and never want to be without you. I hope that's enough for now."

"It is. For as long as you need it to be. As long as I have you beside me it doesn't have to be anything more than it is now." I pull her to my side as we wave good-bye to everyone and head home.

"You deserve someone so much better than me."

"You're all I want or need. Get that through that thick skull of yours. I love you and only you. Forever." I kiss her before shutting her car door. This hard headed woman makes me crazy. But I love it and her.

Chapter 50

"Good morning wife. We really need to find a bigger place to live. AB will be done in a couple of weeks with a current job and could get started on our house if that's something you would like." I walk into the kitchen and kiss her while she's making breakfast then sit on a bar stool awaiting her answer.

"I'm actually okay here. At least for now. I need to get going on my bridal salon and don't want to run the risk of losing a house too if it fails."

"Honey, your bridal salon won't fail. I promise you it won't. Do you want to look at a few possible places today?"

"Yes actually. I was hoping to see the one next to Ella Mae's bakery. From the window it looks perfect." She's getting so excited about this venture and it makes my heart happy.

"Do you have your business name already?" Probably a dumb question since she has been dreaming of this moment since she was five.

"Yes. Zandra's Brides. My mom and I came up with that name when we would dress up my dolls." Her smile is beautiful but sad.

"It is perfect. Let me run to the job site really quick and get everyone started and I will meet you at the space. Let me know when you have the key." We sit down to eat breakfast before I run off to work. I'm actually excited to look at the spaces for her bridal shop too.

***

"The realtor is going to meet us there in ten minutes. If you cannot make it on such short notice I will totally understand." I say to Carter over the phone. I pray he can make it though.

"I will be there. I promised you and honestly I wouldn't miss it for the world. Besides, you need your muscle there to see any fixes that are needed."

"True. I need a contractor not a husband." I smile.

"Good thing you have both. Now I know why you agreed and married me." We both laugh and say our goodbyes.

I'm on a high with excitement of looking at the possible location of Zandra's Brides. And maybe because I get to see Carter too.

I pull up in front of the space for rent and see the realtor must already be here because lights are on inside. And Carter must be inside because there is an AB Construction pickup here also.

I get out and walk inside the building with so much excitement it slips my mind to even look around for the others. I walk around beaming with excitement and hear footsteps coming from the back. I can hear Carter asking questions but when I hear the realtor's voice I freeze. Oh no. Not now.

"Oh there's my wife now. The realtor was just letting me check out the structure before you got here." Carter walks over to me and puts his arm around my waist. He has not noticed yet that I'm still frozen in place.

"Yes, your husband was telling me some of the plans you had. Very exciting. Pretty ambitious though."

"It's going to be great isn't it Zan?" Carter finally looks at me and his own smile fades.

"Hello Zan." Carter looks at the other gentleman and then me questioning what this weird tension is.

"Hello Father. What are you doing here?" I see Carter's head whip around and look at the man he thought was the realtor.

"You're Mr. Carpenter? Why did you let me think you were the realtor this whole time?" Now he's getting mad. I look at my father and see he's quite amused.

"What are you doing here? Where is the realtor we were supposed to be meeting with?" I'm beyond ticked and worried he's going to mess all of this up.

"She was here earlier when I met with her. The space is no longer for sale."

"You didn't. How did you even find out about this?" Who am I kidding he knows everything.

"She called my office for a reference which it was nice of you to use me as one. I had to come see it for myself. And since I was not invited to your wedding young lady I had to come see the man you threw your life away for." He glares at me then Carter. Oh boy, here we go. Not good.

Chapter 51

"Miss Arianna, what would you like to do today?" I ask after Ella Mae leaves. She's not sure what she's doing at our house without her parents or grandma.

"Mama and Dada? Why they no here too?" She's looking around and walks up to Tarley lifting her arms to him. He looks at me questioning this and I motion for him to pick her up.

"Do you want to go to the park before lunch?" Tarley asks after picking her up.

"Park yes. Me go high on swings."

"That sounds like fun. Tarley can probably push you so high you can touch the clouds." Her face lights up with excitement.

"Your dad told me you're a dare devil just like he is. You're definitely his kid." Tarley smiles at me then Arianna and she lays her head on his shoulder melting the big guy's heart. He's going to make such a great dad one of these days. I just hope they are my kids too. Kids? Oh goodness.

"Okay, let's get you changed and ready for the park. Think we can take the pajamas off now?" Ella Mae told us she couldn't get her to put clothes on this morning and we were hoping this would work. But she shakes her head no.

"Pajamas are banned from the park. They are not allowed." Leave it to him to be the bad cop. I smile and take Arianna from his arms.

"Can we put some clothes on and go to the park?"

She looks at Tarley and nods yes. Dang, it worked. Hmmm.

***

"Did you have fun? You went so high you were up in the clouds." Monica is leaning inside her car buckling Arianna into the car seat. And of course I'm checking her out. Haha.

"You can quit staring at my butt. It has not changed since you met me."
She smacks me on the chest when she catches me ogling her.

"It is a great view. You're good with her you know." We both get into
the car and head back to our house.

"Are you making lunch or keeping her busy?" She asks with a
mischievous smile.

"That's a tough one. How about if we go to Sally's."

"That works too. What do you want from Sally's?" She turns and asks
the wiggling little person in the backseat.

"Mac and cheese. Mac and cheese. Mac and cheese." Arianna yells at the
top of her lungs.

"I think she wants mac and cheese Mon. Do they even have that on the
menu?"

"Goodness I sure hope so."

We pull up at Sally's and go through the unfamiliar song and dance of
getting a child out of the car with all her stuff. My goodness it takes an
army.

***

Norma comes over to our table with menus and a piping hot bowl of mac
and cheese. They must come here a lot if they know before we even sat
down what Arianna wanted.

"You're my hero." I say and smile appreciatively at Norma.

"Mother of four and grandmother of six. Plus, she always has a
meltdown if she has to wait long."

"But we just got here. How did you do that so fast?"

"Lizzie told us to watch for you guys. We saw you pull up and started it then."

"Once again, you're my hero. I feel so inadequate with her. Thank you." She pats my shoulder and takes our order.

"They knew we wouldn't cook. How nice." Tarley frowns.

"No, she will only eat our mac and cheese most days so they have to come in even if it is only to get hers." Norma says when she brings our drinks.

"So it's not us? That's good to know."

"You will get the hang of it and want a couple of your own." She winks at me then smiles at Tarley. I think he blushes. He must be thinking about how babies are made. Such a typical man.

I shake my head at him and he blushes again before asking. "What?"

"As if you're that innocent."

Chapter 52

"You need to sign this paperwork." My father says to Carter once everyone has been introduced. I'm still in shock that he came here but not in shock about the dirty trick he's pulling with the space for my bridal salon.

"What is it? It better not be a prenup Dad." I see him set his briefcase down and retrieve some documents from it. He hands them to Carter with a fake smile.

"If you expect me to accept you as my son in law then you need to sign this paperwork preventing you from draining any and all monies my daughter may have."

"Father. This is unwarranted. Carter is not after my money. Unlike your wives after Mother." I spit out and glare.

"If and when you decide you don't want to be married to my dear daughter I want to ensure you won't get anything from her that's not yours to take."

"He's not signing that. Never. You wasted a trip coming here for this. He will never sign it. Go home and forget this." Carter looks at me and I shake my head. No way am I letting him sign that paper just to give Dad what he wants.

"If you want this space for your new bridal shop you will allow him to sign it."

"You have got to be kidding me. I lose out on my space because you're mad and want to punish me? Well you know what? I'm not a child. I'm this man's wife and there is nothing you can do about it." I grab my purse and Carter's hand before storming out.

"Who the Hell does he think he is? How dare he blackmail us like that?"

"Zan, what are you going to do about a shop now? You had your heart set on this one." He takes me in his arms and holds me tight.

Just as I'm about to relax I catch a figure to my left and know who it is and what look is on his face. He thinks he's going to win this one. He's not.

***

Before I can get into my work pickup and follow Zan home her father walks up to me and hands me a business card.

"What's this for?" I look at him curious as to what he's up to now. I'm so upset and it is taking all the control I have not to punch him right in the face.

"When you're ready to talk, give me a call. I will be here until this evening. You know what you need to do."

Unbelievable. No wonder Zandra's the way she is. This man is a force to be reckoned with. I have a feeling he's going to get his way too. Even if Zan is so against it.

I call Maysen needing some advice. I'm in uncharted territory and have no clue what to do.

"Hey man, what's up?"

"Maysen, I need some advice."

"Trouble in paradise already? That didn't take long."

"Shut up. It's nothing like that. Zan's dad showed up today and is demanding I sign a prenup or he's not going to let her buy the store space she's wanting." I tell him every detail of what happened and even he's quiet afterwards.

"Wow. That man sounds intimidating. What are you going to do?"

"Part of me knows I need to do as Zandra wishes but I also want to prove to her father that I'm not after the money. I also know how much her heart was set on that space. I mean come on, I'm the one causing all of this conflict."

"Not really. Her dad seems like a controlling nightmare and is used to getting his way."

"Very much so. I wonder if I can talk to him and get him to change his mind and even apologize to her?"

"That's playing with fire."

"He has hurt her for her entire life. Maybe I can get him to see that and things can be better between them."

"Are you stupid? This is going to blow up in your face. I'm not sure who will be more ticked off."

"I've got to try. Thanks man."

"Your funeral. Good luck. You're going to need it. A lot of it."

He's right I'm going to need it.

***

"That man is unreasonable. But what's new? He has been this way my entire life." I'm pacing in the realtor's office having a mini meltdown. "Isn't there anything you can do? I asked to see the place first. Doesn't that mean anything?"

"I'm sorry but in our business money talks. Whoever shows up with the funding first wins. I'm so sorry. I had no Earthly idea he was your dad."

"I cannot believe this. I've been looking through that front window for a month. That's the main reason I decided to move here and start the shop. Everything was contingent on that building."

"I would be happy to show you some other spaces. Maybe you will find one even better." Poor lady is trying to make things better but my hissy fit probably made her think I'm a lunatic.

"Yes please. Maybe you're right. When God closes one door he opens another. Right?" I smile at her and smooth my hair.

"The first space is across the street from here actually."

"My husband is going to have to miss these ones but I'm ready. I can always show him before we make a decision." And before I waste his time again. Good grief he's probably wishing he hadn't have married me now. How humiliating. Dad walked around with Carter sizing him up without Carter even knowing who he was. What a jerk.

Chapter 53

"Ready for bed little terror?" I hear Tarley ask Arianna when we get back into the living room.

"She has had her bath, dinner, and drink of water. She's all set for a bedtime story aren't you?" Arianna climbs onto Tarley's lap once again melting his heart. I can tell by the look on his face that he's touched.

"Story?" She asks sweetly and looks up at him.

"Of course. Let's go get you in bed and we will read the story in there. Okay?" She smiles and lays her head on his shoulder when he stands up.

The sight of them makes my biological clock start ticking at a rapid pace. Maybe I am ready for a family. Who knew?

Ten minutes later Tarley comes back into the living room looking exhausted.

"She wanted four stories. Thank goodness she crashed after three. She's a whirlwind. Dang I'm completely exhausted!" He sits down next to me and lays his head back on the cushion. I wouldn't be surprised if he starts snoring.

"Ready for bed too? She will probably be up early again."

"Can we watch a movie in bed?" He smiles at me making it impossible to tell him no.

"As long as you hold me through the whole thing."

***

"Uncle Tarley?" I awake to what I think is someone calling my name. Please don't be a nightmare. I look over at Monica and she's sleeping peacefully. Wasn't her.

Then I feel the soft hand touch my arm. It is then I realize it was Arianna who was calling my name. Oh goodness I hope I didn't wake her up with a nightmare. I don't remember having one though.

"Uncle Tarley? Uncle Tarley?"

"What is it sweetheart?" I lean over and lay my hand on top of hers.

"I had a nightmare. And my dada said if I did to come get you. You have them too." Ah poor baby.

"Yes honey I do. Let's go get a drink before we wake up Monica." I get out of bed and Arianna grabs my hand while we walk to the kitchen.

I get us both a small glass and fill it with water.

"Thank you. I was so thirsty from being scared." She sets her empty glass down and looks at me.

"Wanna talk about the nightmare? It helps me to talk to Monica about mine."

"I don't member it just waked me up because it scared me. You mad cause I waked you up?"

"Of course not. If anyone knows how to deal with the nightmares it would be me. Wanna rock in the chair for a few minutes before going back to bed?" She smiles that angelic smile and we rock in the chair for a little while.

***

It is almost six-thirty in the morning and I cannot find Tarley. He must have had another nightmare and slept on the couch afterwards. I peek in the spare room looking in on Arianna but her bed is empty too. Surely they aren't up already.

I walk into the living room expecting to see them eating cereal and watching cartoons. But instead what I find sends my heart in a flutter. Tarley is sitting in the rocking chair sound asleep with Arianna wrapped in his arms also asleep. Aww. What are they out here for? Maybe I will lay here on the couch and read until they wake up. I don't want to interrupt this amazing moment.

After a few chapters I hear the rocking chair creak which catches my attention. Looking over there I see a big strong man enamored by a little girl that's fast asleep in his arms.

"My arms are asleep. Help."

"Here I will take her back to her bed." I lift her out of his arms. The smile on his face makes my heart do flips. Seems like we need to have a very important conversation. Sooner rather than later.

Chapter 54

"So glad you came to your senses son."

"Mr. Carpenter we need to have a talk. A serious talk before I sign anything."

"I knew you wanted money. You can fool my daughter but not me."

"I don't want your money."

"Then what do you want? You came out here just to share our feelings and what? Do crafts together?"

"Very funny sir. I came out here because I want things to be better between my wife and her father."

"Better? Things are fine."

"Right. That's why you had to find out from someone else about her wedding."

"We are not close but it is just the way it has always been."

"Since her mother died. I know. She has told me all about her life. She also told me how unimportant she is to you. How absent you are in her life. And how much it hurts her." His face turns a little pale at those final words.

"She told you that? She thinks she's unimportant to me? She's the most important thing."

"Have you ever told her that? When is the last time you told her you loved her and were proud of her?"

That might have been a little far when his face turns to stone again and scowls.

"Son did you come here today to sign this prenup? I have a plane waiting over there and business to tend to." Wow just like he's back to normal and not phased at all.

"I will sign anything you want. I care about your daughter and she cannot know I signed it. She will be furious with us both."

"You seriously want to sign?" He doesn't know whether to believe me or not.

"I would do anything for Zan. Even if that means doing something she's going to be furious at me for to make her dreams come true."

"You love her?" Wow to the point.

"Yes I do. I wouldn't be here trying to make a deal with the devil if I didn't love her. She wants that store space and if signing this prenup will get it for her then give me a pen."

"Hmmm you might be an honorable man who really does love my daughter after all." He rips up the paperwork and smiles at me. Yes, he's smiling instead of glaring. Interesting.

"I do sir. I'm serious about signing that."

"I believe you. I'm going to go against my every instinct here and not expect the prenup. Please don't make me or my daughter regret this." He turns and strides to the waiting jet. He climbs the small steps but pauses before entering the cabin.

"Take care of my little girl." And he disappears inside while the steps fold up.

I stand watching my father-in-law leave in a jet bigger than my apartment building and feel a little uneasy about what comes next. I didn't sign the document so she cannot be mad at me. Right?

***

"Hi babe. Did your day get any better?" Carter says when he comes in the front door. I'm about finished with dinner feeling defeated but happy to see him.

"A little. We looked at a few more spaces but they were either too big, too small, or needed a ton of work before I could even move stuff in." He gives me a hug and kisses the top of my head. I try my hardest not to sigh.

"Well, we could always build exactly what you want. Might take a few months though."

"I will find something that will work. She has two more to show me in the morning. Hopefully they are going to work."

"I'm sorry the one you wanted didn't work out. I had no idea that was your dad either. I about choked on my tongue when you called him father." He laughs. I cannot help but laugh myself because I can only imagine how crazy that whole situation was for him.

"I know. He was the last person I ever expected to show up there. And trying to force you to sign that prenup? Oh I was ready to knock him out!"

"It will all work out. I'm just sorry he hurt you again." He wraps me up in his arms again just as the doorbell rings.

Ding dong.

I look up at Carter and find he's looking down at me in question too.

"I'm not expecting anyone. I'm sure my father is back in Charlotte by now counting his money."

"I will get it." I make trips to the dining table with the lasagna and garlic bread I made but Carter goes to answer the door.

He opens it and we are both surprised to see the realtor standing outside the apartment.

I put the plate of bread down and walk to her.

"What's going on? Let me guess he bought all the properties for sale in this entire town?" I say sarcastically but honestly wouldn't put it past him.

"I came to drop off the paperwork for the sale of the property you wanted originally."

"I don't understand. I thought he bought it already?"

"He did. But it is in your name. You own that building yourself. There is also this letter that came with the paperwork." She hands me a file full of papers and then a simple white envelope.

I look at Carter as he thanks her and shuts the front door. He smiles and waits for me to open it.

"I don't know what's going on but it sounds wonderful."

I open the envelope to find a handwritten letter from my dad. Hmm never gotten one of these before.

Zandra darling,

First I want to tell you that I'm so proud of the woman you have become. I'm always blown away by the ferocity that is my daughter.

If you're reading this letter that means you have gotten the paperwork on your bridal shop. I'm not sure if you have ever received enough love and affection from me over the years so I hope this grand gesture will help make things better. Please forgive me for all the hurt I've caused.

You found a fine young man that you have taken as your husband. I like him. Let's just say he's a much better man than I am and I'm proud to call him son, too. I'm very happy for you two and wish you all the love and happiness.

Come see me sometime. I miss you. Good luck with your business and please never hesitate to contact me if you need anything.

I love you,

Your father

Chapter 55

Ding dong.

Tarley and I look at each other when we hear the doorbell with relief on our faces. Ella Mae is here to get Arianna. It has been two very long days.

"Gramma." She yells and runs to the door. Tarley and I would probably do the same if it wouldn't make us look like lunatics.

"Hi sweet girl. Were you good for Monica and Tarley? I missed you so much." She picks Arianna up and snuggles her close.

"She was perfect. How was your trip?" I smile at Tarley then Ella Mae.

"It was great. Savannah and the kids are always a sight for sore eyes. Speaking of sore eyes, you two look exhausted." She laughs. Dang she noticed how ragged we feel.

"Let's just say we are not used to having a child with so much energy around. We loved having her here with us though." I hand Ella Mae the bags we had for Arianna and kiss the little one on the forehead.

"See you later sweetie. Thanks for staying with us."

"You take care of your grandma okay? Bye bye." He also kisses her forehead before they turn and go.

As soon as the door is shut we both breathe a big sigh of relief. Oh my goodness we made it and she's gone. Hallelujah for the peace and quiet.

***

The instant the door shuts I slump down on the couch ready to take a twenty-four-hour nap.

"That was the most exhausting two days of my life." I say to Monica as she joins me on the couch.

"I think I could sleep for a week. She was a lot of fun though. The house is going to feel empty without her running around like a wild child." We both laugh.

"For sure. And we don't have to make mac and cheese ever again."

"And you won't have to sleep in the rocking chair again."

"I didn't mind that. She had that nightmare and we were only going to rock for a few minutes. But it put me to sleep too."

"It was the sweetest thing to find that morning. It is so quiet right now."

"We could bring our own baby into this house." Did I seriously just say that?

"I would rather adopt. I think there are too many kids out there without homes. I want to have kids with you but adopting seems the best way.

"Hmm. I would never have thought of that actually but I agree with you. Adopting our children will be rewarding in other ways than just becoming parents."

"So we agree? Do you really want to look into adopting a child with me?" She sits up straight on the couch no longer exhausted but very excited.

***

"I don't see why not. We are both employed and have a lot to offer a child. You figure out what needs to be done and where we go from here." We are going to adopt a child. Oh my goodness I cannot believe it; I'm going to be a mother.

"I'm so excited Tarley. I've never been one who wanted to experience pregnancy or labor so this will be amazing. Do you want a certain age?"

"No. I'm not picky. As long as the child is healthy then I'll be over the moon. I'm going to be a father." He smiles at me and my insides do flips. I love this man so much. And now we are going to be parents.

"I will call around today and see how we get this process started. Are you going to work now?"

"Yes. We have another mama ready to have her baby."

"Which one this time?" I wish I didn't have to work so I could see another baby born.

"April Showers. Don't ask because I have no idea who named her that or why."

"Are you going to name the baby May Flowers?" I laugh at my own ridiculous joke. He's not laughing.

"Yes, Amelia has declared that its name will be that so she can always say April Showers brought May Flowers. As lame as that sounds." He's frowning definitely not finding any amusement in this.

"Oh, it's cute. Quit being a grump." I kiss him and go get ready for work while he leaves for the 6AB. I can hear him still grumbling on about how dumb those names are. Haha I love them.

Chapter 56

"This place is absolutely perfect Carter. Don't you think? The dress forms will go along there. The racks over there and my sewing machine over here."

"Sounds perfect babe. I'm so glad your dad came through."

"Came through? What's that supposed to mean?" Oh boy I did it now. Open mouth, insert foot. Crap.

"Um I met with him the night he was here at the airport before he flew back to Charlotte." I'm afraid to look at her.

"You didn't. Please Carter tell me you didn't sign that damned prenup he had."

"I didn't. I went with the intention to trade this space for it but after our little talk he tore up the documents before having me sign them."

"Little talk? Do I even want to know what this talk was about?"

"You. I just told him that I was more than willing to sign those papers if he was willing to let you have your dream space. I told him to let you buy it but I guess he had an even bigger change of heart." Well, her face isn't as red as it was. That's a good sign, right?

"What did you say to him exactly? That letter said things I've never heard from that man."

"I told him just what I thought of how he treats you and how much he has hurt you." Oh crap her face is red again. And she's not saying anything.

"Zan talk to me. I'm sorry if you're mad at me but I had to talk to him. It was my one and only chance to be real with him."

"I don't really know what to say. On one hand I'm ticked at you for going without telling me but on the other I'm so touched. No one has ever stood up to him before." Tears start to form in her eyes which is my que to go to her. I wrap my arms around her waist and lay my head on top of hers.

"I love you Zan and I would do anything to see you happy. Even sign a prenup if you wanted me to."

"You love me?" She looks up at me in shock. The thought of her not knowing how I feel about her hits hard.

"Of course I do. I didn't marry you just to tick off your dad. You're the one person I want to be with every moment of every day."

***

This incredible man loves me. I had no idea. Yes, I knew he cared but not like that.

"Carter I've loved you since the gas station fiasco when you were my knight in shining armor and I was hooked."

"I would rescue you any day. I've been searching for that one person I was meant for and was honestly convinced she didn't exist. Until Lizzie brought you here to rescue her wedding." Awe wow heart melting.

"Then I met the town bad boy and got hooked on his easy going charms. I could tell from our first meeting that there was a lot more to you than being a player. Liz warned me a million times to stay away but I couldn't and I thank God that Jonathan sent us to Colorado. It was there that I knew without a doubt you were the one."

"Now you're stuck with me until I die. That was not very romantic, sorry." We both laugh and he kisses me without any cares in the world.

***

"So, when do you wanna take our little trip?" Smooth change of subject idiot.

"You wanna go? I was hoping you did. After the letter and getting this place for me I feel like I need to thank him in person."

"I agree. I'll book us tickets for Friday night and come home Sunday. Does that work?"

"I'll get the Carpenter jet here so we can ride in comfort at whatever time we're ready."

"Seriously? I'm not sure I've ever been on one of those."

"He said if I needed anything and he always hates it when I fly commercial. You better get used to the perks of being married to a Carpenter." She gives me a wicked smile.

"I'm in for a wild ride aren't I?" I kiss her once more and thank my lucky stars for this woman. What more could I ask for? I can only think of one thing.

Someday man, someday.

Chapter 57

"So April Showers brought May Flowers today?" I tease when he comes in the door.

"Oh shut up. Quit saying those ridiculous names. But yes, the baby was born about an hour ago." He grimaces and shakes his head. All I can do is laugh.

"Oh, it could be worse you know." I rub his shoulders while he sits down to remove his boots.

"You're in a good mood. What gives?"

"I talked to the adoption agency in Tulsa today. We have a ton of paperwork to fill out but besides that she said she would get the ball rolling."

"That fast?"

"She said since we didn't expect a newborn this first time it wouldn't take as long. That's if our background checks, home visits and all that checks out okay."

"Geez. They want more than the Army did when I enlisted."

"Yes. Are you sure about this?" I look at him afraid he's having second thoughts.

"No. Not at all. Just surprised at all they need. But I'm sure it is warranted so they don't place kids with awful people."

"I'm sure it happens still. But after dinner we can start filling them out if you're ready."

"Sure. Let me eat first. Going to need my strength for all that paperwork." We both laugh but sit down to dinner.

"My goodness Mon I'm going to gain fifty pounds with your cooking."

"Well, things are about to bet busier at AB so I won't be cooking extravagant meals then. I'm just spoiling you now."

"I like to be spoiled. How are things going at work?"

"Good. We just finished up a job and picked up another. Mrs. Styne has that storm repair still needing done too. And Carter's been MIA a lot lately so at least I've been able to avoid his drama."

"He and Zandra still married? They looked pretty happy at the wedding reception."

"Yes as far as I know. Jonathan's gone now for another week and a half but we've got enough guys to cover. They have to answer to me a little more but that's no big deal."

"You're bossy every day so I'm sure it works out." He smiles and we continue on with small talk.

***

I hear my phone ringing from the kitchen so I run to answer before Monica wakes up. I look at the clock when I get there and it says 2:15 AM. What? I look and see it is Jonathan. Oh crap.

"What's wrong man?"

"Oh crap dude I didn't even realize it was so late."

"What's going on? Why are you calling me from your honeymoon?"

"I couldn't wait to tell you the good news. I've been laying here and had to call."

"What news man?'

"We are pregnant."

"Wow congrats. Arianna's going to love being a big sister."

"I'm so happy. I will get to be around for all of it this time."

"I know that will be awesome for you guys. While you're on the line I will tell you our good news."

"Mon's pregnant too?"

"No. We have decided to seek adoption. We actually filled out all the paperwork a couple of days ago."

"Ah man that's perfect for you two! Dads together! So cool. Okay I better get back to bed. You too. Happy for you bud!"

"You too. See you later." Wow they are having another baby. And we are trying to get a child. Everything seems to be working out perfectly.

Chapter 58

Nine months later…

Zandra's Brides has been open a few months shy of a year and we've been non-stop busy. Between Amie Blake's wedding planning and our dresses, Colvin's wedding scene is covered. Brides are coming from all over which means the world to me.

"Well, that's the last wedding on the books before the big one. Since it's next month we have a lot of little details to wrap up and the last fitting's in three weeks." I tell my assistant Laura.

"Monica and Tarley are going to be in today at four to do the final choices for the colors. What time is your appointment?" She smiles at me and without thinking about it I put my hands on my growing baby bump.

"Two thirty. I should be back in plenty of time. It is our second ultrasound and hopefully we can tell the sex this time."

Yep, Carter and I are expecting our first child in two months. We cannot be any more excited to see what he or she looks like. After seeing Lizzie's new baby boy I'm not sure which one I would like more. My father wants a boy he can groom to take over Carpenter Enterprises but Carter and I don't share that vision for this child.

My dad has been spending a lot more time with us here in Colvin than he has at home in Charlotte. His most recent marriage fell apart because of it but none of us were surprised. Carter seems to think Dad is going to sell all of his business assets and retire to Colvin but I'm not sure he could handle living without all of it. Or that we could handle it. That makes me smile because he would drive us all insane if he didn't have all that power and those people to boss around.

"I'm going to run out for a quick lunch. Need anything while I'm out?"

"No, I'm okay. Carter will be by in a few minutes I'm sure. He hovers like a mother hen." We both laugh knowing he's exactly like that too.

"Alright. Be back later. Call me if you need anything."

"Go. Aren't I the boss here?" She smiles and waves on her way out the door.

As she gets in her car I see her waving to someone and then I see his handsome face. My heart kicks up a beat and I cannot help but smile.

"Hi honey. How is your day so far?" He kisses me hello and kisses my stomach.

"Not bad. I saw Laura leaving on my way in. I'm sure glad you found her. She's great."

"That she is. When I'm on maternity leave this place will be in excellent hands."

"That it will. Think we will be able to see if this baby is a boy or a girl today?"

"Hope so. Little buggar has not cooperated as of yet."

"Tarley asked me to be one of the groomsmen today. I think he's pretty nervous."

"Bet you're glad ours was so low key."

"Absolutely. George and Wilma are flying in next Friday to Tulsa. I will leave right after lunch to go get them."

"Very nice. I cannot wait to see them. I miss them."

"I know, me too. We really lucked out when we found them. They have adopted me like I was their son in turn loving you just as much. Crazy how this world works."

"This baby is going to have an amazing two grandpas and one grandma. Very blessed." I put my hands on my stomach just in time to feel the baby kick. I must have smiled when it happened because Carter steps forward and puts his hands there too.

"Whoa that's a big one. Man. I sure hope we can find out which one it is today. I'm tired of calling the baby an it." He laughs.

"Lizzie thinks it's a boy, but that could be because she just had Dalton. She has this fantasy of our boys growing up together and being best friends."

"Even if it is a girl they still can. Look at Aiden and Karlie."

"Oh that's true."

***

"Zandra Greene?" We hear being called that afternoon while waiting in the lobby of the doctor's office.

I squeeze Zan's hand and she smiles at me nervously. We both would like to know the sex of this baby but aren't too confident that we will be able to tell.

"Doctor will be with you shortly. Then I will bring in the machine and we will hopefully be able to see whether we have a boy or a girl." The nurse tells us and exits the room.

I look over at Zandra and she's almost in tears. "What's wrong babe?"

"Just emotional. I really want to know the gender Carter. I might cry if the baby won't let us see this time either." I kiss her forehead and hug her lightly.

"Babe I think you're going to cry either way." That makes her laugh and temporarily takes her mind off of it. I hold her until the doctor comes in and finishes the exam.

"Everything looks great. They will bring the ultrasound machine in now so we can see how everything is going inside."

"And whether we are having a daughter or a son, I hope." Zan says and we all laugh.

"This sure has been a stubborn one when it has come to revealing the sex." He chuckles and shakes my hand on his way out.

"It is time for some answers. You ready?" She nods trying not to cry again.

"Hello Zandra and Carter. Doctor says everything looks good. Let's see if the baby wants to reveal its gender today."

I watch the technician squirt the jelly on Zan's stomach. When she starts to move the control around on that spot I get butterflies.

"Please baby let us see what you are going to be." I say and Zan squeezes my hand hard. Almost too hard leaving not much feeling in it.

"Well, well, well. I think the baby heard you. You sure you want to know? Last chance." I look down at Zan to find she has sat up almost all the way and looking at the screen hoping to see for herself.

"Yes!" We yell excitedly at the same time.

"Well, you're carrying your son. It's a boy. Congratulations."

Zandra bursts into uncontrollable sobs and covers her face with her hands.

"Did you not want a son Zandra? I'm sorry you're disappointed." Poor technician is feeling terrible about my crazy pregnant wife crying her eyes out. I smile and pat Zandra on the head.

"We are thrilled. We didn't care which but she has been very emotional today. Thank you so much."

The baffled technician smiles and wheels the machine out of the room. She probably couldn't get away from us fast enough.

"You freaked that poor lady out Zan. Are you okay?" I lean down and kiss her forehead.

"Oh my goodness, I'm so glad we know what the baby is now." She wipes away the tears and sits up again. Her eyes and face are so red it looks like she was hit by a truck.

"For sure. We can call the baby by his name now."

She smiles and lays her hands on the baby bump.

"Yep. We can now call him Wyatt Carter George Greene."

Oh my goodness hearing the baby's official name fills my whole body with warmth.

"Yep. Your dad's middle name, mine, my adopted dad's name and of course our last name. Think he can handle such a long and powerful name?" We both laugh.

"I'm sure he will be an amazing young man just like his father. Thank you for loving me Carter. You're the best quick decision I've ever made. I love you."

"You were the best thing that has ever happened to me. Until this baby. He's a definite close second. Love you Zan. Our future looks so bright."

"We can do anything as long as we are together."

Chapter 59

"Tarley I'm going to take Sasha to Ella Mae's while we go to Zandra's. She'll be bored out of her mind at the shop and this way she can play with Arianna." He comes out of the bedroom ready for work and smiles at me. He's getting a late start this morning.

"What? What are you smiling at me for?" Just about that moment when his expression turned to a whole other emotion, Sasha comes barreling out of her bedroom.

"Dad, can I take my ponies to Awiana house?" Tarley picks our daughter up and kisses her forehead before nodding yes.

Yes, the adoption process was a huge success. Two months after we filled out the paperwork this little green-eyed brunette came to us. She was just a little over two years old but had never had a forever home before. We were ecstatic to be able to provide that and so much more for her.

She and Arianna are only a few months apart and they bonded the very first time they met. While she still asks once in a while if we are going to keep her even after we have a baby like Lizzie did, we explain to her that she's our baby and we are not sure if she will get a sibling or not. We make sure and explain that we won't be getting a baby or sibling for her the way everyone does but will come like she did. When she's tired and scared she will ask us if we are her forever mommy and daddy, which we say yes. She's our gift from God and no one will ever keep us apart. For the most part she's adjusted and doesn't really remember not being with us. We pray that over time she will completely forget. She's also over the moon excited that Tarley and I are getting married next month so she can be the flower girl. She thinks throwing the petals on the ground will be a lot of fun. Let's just hope she doesn't throw them at people as she walks down the aisle.

"You have to eat with Mommy and take a little nap before you can go see Arianna." Tarley tells her getting a dirty look back.

"Maybe you need one now Miss Priss." He sits her down and slides her plate of breakfast closer. She looks at the contents and wrinkles her nose. She's not a fan of eggs so I'm trying to cover them with cheese but she's not fooled.

"Yuck. Eggs. I don't have to eat?" Looking up at me with a sweet smile, she's clearly trying to work the system.

"Four bites." I think there is only four there but she still whines and shoves every single piece of egg in her mouth.

"Well, she won that round." Tarley laughs and kisses me goodbye.

"Did she? I do believe she ate all her eggs." I smile and stick my tongue out at him.

"Okay you both won. Goodness I sure hope we get another male in this house soon to even up the score."

I throw the dishtowel at him making Sasha laugh out loud.

***

"Hey guys. Thanks for coming. We have a few things to decide on today. Are you ready?" Zandra asks us when we get to her bridal store. She and Amie are both meeting us here for us to make some final wedding decisions. I would rather shut my hand in a car door than be here but Monica gets so happy when I agree to go to these appointments.

"Tarley we have a treat for you today. Ella Mae brought samples for you two to try." Amie says with a knowing smile.

"Now we are talking! This decision I can handle!" Everyone laughs as I rub my hands together ready to eat some cake.

"What color of tuxes did you decide on for all of the guys?" Monica asks making me wait to devour this tray of goodies. I frown at her and she smiles. Typical.

"No tux. Dark jeans, white dress shirt and gray vest." I say as I look at Monica praying she's still okay with the casual attire.

"That will be more like you and will be perfect. I'm sure the guys will be happy too. Monica's dress has been started also and after a few more details this wedding will be on its way." Zandra says while flipping through a binder. I think these women call it "The Wedding Binder."

"Centerpieces? Did you decide?" Amie asks Monica.

"White candles with white ribbon tied around the outside and we can't forget about the daisies."

"Can we start on the cake yet? I'm going to fall asleep soon." I smile and the ladies all laugh shaking their heads.

***

"Chocolate cake with raspberry filling and raspberry buttercream frosting tinted yellow. Dark jeans, white shirts, no ties, and grey vests. Candles, white ribbon and daisies. White table cloths with yellow runners. Does that sound about right?" Zandra looks up from her notes and smiles. She's such a beautiful pregnant woman.

"Perfect. Now, tell us what you found out this afternoon."

"It's a boy!" She screams and claps her hands. She's clearly very excited. Her excitement makes me smile and I stand up to meet her for a hug.

"Awe! How exciting. I bet Carter is over the moon! He told me he was certain it was a boy."

"Yes, he's very happy about it but we both just pray this baby will be healthy. We can have a girl next time for mommy." She beams.

"Sasha has been asking for a little brother a lot more since Lizzie had Dalton. We're thinking after the wedding maybe we can start the process again."

"Is she excited to wear her princess dress in the wedding?"

"Oh yes. She asks every morning if I will let her wear it even for a second." We both laugh.

"Kids are so funny. I remember Arianna wearing her dress every day for months after Jonathan and Lizzie's wedding."

"I remember we had a heck of a time getting her to take it off and bathe!"

***

"Do you have all that's needed from me ladies?" I speak up to remind them I'm still here amid their girl talk.

"Yes Tarley we do. Thank you for suffering through. This will be the last one. The rest will be small details along the way that can be taken care of over the phone."

"Well, thank you for seeing us and congrats on the baby boy. I will have to give Carter a call. Take care. I will see you at home Babe. I'll pick Sasha up before I go home." I kiss Monica goodbye and wave to the other ladies in the shop.

Whew that was excruciating! The cake was worth it though. I feel like I can breathe again. I need to go drink a beer or something to get some masculinity back. My wife to be would have called me a pig for that comment. Haha.

I drive to Ella Mae's house to pick up Sasha and am happy to see Jonathan and Carter are there too.

"Your mom moves into a one-bedroom apartment to get away from the likes of you and you come bother her there too?"

I see Jonathan flip me off behind Arianna's back and Carter laughs out loud.

"Oh I love to see my boy. Don't you listen to them honey." She smiles wide and winks at me.

"Daddy! Daddy!" Sasha comes running up to me and when I pick her up it makes my heart sing. I love being a daddy.

"Heard about the baby. Congrats! I bet you were excited to hear it is a boy."

"Very. I mean I would have been more than happy with a girl too but of course a son is what I was hoping for. What man doesn't?"

"I'm hoping we get the call someday to tell us there is a little boy out there that needs a family. Mon says after the wedding but I would take that call any day." I kiss Sasha on the head and smile.

"I've gotta go relieve my wife from baby duty for a bit. I will see you all soon. Take care." Jonathan says and leaves with Arianna toddling after him. Our lives sure have changed.

"Alright I've gotta go force my wife to go home. She has been working around the clock to get all loose ends wrapped up before the baby comes."

"I just left there and she was blowing and going. But Mon was there with her still too. Good luck getting that pow-wow split up."

"See ya man." Sasha and I head for the pickup and make our way home. I had better get dinner started because I'm sure Monica hasn't left the bridal store yet. Get those women together and you will be there for hours. Once again it is crazy how different our lives are now.

A daughter. Wedding a month away. Possible son on the way.

Completely different from U.S. Army and Afghanistan. No bullets or war.

Thankfully it is night and day different. Thank you Lord.

Chapter 60

A few weeks later….

"Nervous?" I hear Jonathan ask from the doorway of the barn on the 6AB. When I look over at him I see that Carter and Aaron are also with him.

My closest friends. Never in a million years would I have thought I'd live in a small town and have such wonderful people in my life. Yes, I've known Jonathan for most of my life but thanks to him I've also gotten to know these gentlemen.

And most importantly my wife to be.

"Not at all. I'm feeling extremely grateful that I made that quick trip to come and see you. This place and all of you guys have changed my life. Thank you all." I lift a glass of whiskey up and so do the other men.

"We all feel the same way man. But you do realize you're sounding like a girl, right?" Carter jokes before downing his whole drink.

"Let's do this then, I'm ready to kiss my wife for the first time." I quickly swallow the remainder of my whiskey and set the glass down.

They all pat me on the back as I lead the way out of the tack room where I've been getting ready.

We decided to have the wedding in the exact same spot where I planned our first date. It's a nighttime ceremony so Monica had it recreated with candles to look just like it did that night. Amelia and AJ were thrilled.

I walk down the pathway lined with flickering candles and look from side to side at the amazing people that are here to witness Monica and myself exchange vows. My heart is so full of love right now and my eyes feel as if they could start leaking any moment.

Better wait until I see the love of my life first.

***

"It's time Mon. You ready for this?" Aaron asks from the doorway of the living room in the 6AB's main house. He's smiling at me and looks so happy.

"I sure am. Have you seen Tarley?"

"Yep. Just had a drink with him and the groomsmen before they walked to the altar. He's ready and waiting."

"Is he doing okay? He's not nervous or ready to back out is he?"

"Calm down Mon. He's at the end of that aisle waiting for the love of his life. That's you, remember?"

"Yes, I'm so afraid this is just a dream."

"I will pinch you if you need me to." He laughs.

"You would. Okay I'm ready. Thank you for walking me down the aisle."

"You're one of my best friends and like my little sister. Of course I'm honored to walk you down the aisle. Thank you for asking me to."

When we step outside the house we see that Sasha and Arianna are starting down the path throwing flower petals down as they go.

"Awe. They look like little princesses."

"And one of them is your little princess." He takes my arm in his and starts towards the candle lit pathway.

I cannot believe I'm actually getting married. And to the most amazing man I've ever met. My heart is so full as I begin the slow walk towards my future husband.

My husband, wow.

"He has tears running down his cheeks at the sight of you. He loves you so much." Aaron smiles over at me while I try to keep myself from falling apart. There are so many emotions running through me that I'm not sure which to hang onto.

Love. I will hang onto that. I do love this man, that little girl and all of these people here tonight.

***

"She looks so beautiful." I say to myself when Monica comes out of the shadows with Aaron by her side. She absolutely takes my breath away. I knew she would be stunning but this is even more than I imagined. I don't know if it's the candle light or what but holy smokes.

I wipe away a few tears as she draws nearer and nearer. My heart is racing faster with every step they take. I think I'm going to have a heart attack before she gets up here.

Then she smiles at me and all that anxiety fades away. This woman knows just what I need at the exact moment I need it. She was definitely made for me.

Aaron and Monica finally reach the end of the aisle and I take her hand in mine. She smiles again and I feel at peace and at home.

"Dearly beloved we are gathered here today to witness the joining of Tarley Wilson and Monica Evans."

That's all I remember because after that I stood looking into Monica's eyes and the rest of the world faded away.

***

"Congratulations Mr. and Mrs. Wilson. It was a beautiful ceremony. You look marvelous too." Amie says to us at the reception. She's carrying a baby in each arm both sound asleep.

"Oh they are just so sweet. How do you do it with two?"

"Aaron helps a lot. Amelia and all the girls come help too."

"They are so sweet. Definitely worth the double headaches."

"When they are sleeping they are the sweetest things. Abbie is the quiet one, but Alec has a set of lungs on him." We all laugh trying not to wake the babies.

"If you need a break let us know. We are going to hopefully be getting another child soon. We probably could use the practice with more than one."

"I will remember that. Enjoy the rest of your night."

"Well, Mrs. Wilson how are you feeling?" Tarley asks as he wraps me up in his arms. He keeps trying to do this but gets interrupted each time.

"So good to see you two happy." And there is the interruption. We turn to see Amelia and AJ standing in front of us grinning from ear to ear.

"Thank you so much for allowing us to have the wedding and reception here. It turned out so much better than I dreamed it would." I say and hug each one.

"You're more than welcome. You're family. Don't forget that." We watch them walk away while Zandra and Carter walk towards us.

"If I say you look beautiful will you think I'm hitting on you?" We all laugh because a year ago it might have caused an issue but it is so great how close we have all become.

"I know better than to think you're hitting on me." Tarley says and we all bust up laughing again.

"This wedding and the dresses turned out beyond my wildest dreams. I cannot thank you enough." I hug Zandra the best I can with her swollen stomach.

"You're more than welcome. I enjoyed it and now I can go on maternity leave knowing everyone is happy. I'm so ready to have this baby." We seem to be hearing that first part from everyone tonight.

"We cannot wait to meet him. Let us know if you need anything any time." We watch them walk away with Zandra holding her stomach.

"I'm so thankful my kids came without that part." We laugh and walk to get a drink. As we are doing so we get stopped by Maysen and Audrey who have their son Abbott with them.

"Congratulations guys. It was a beautiful wedding." Audrey says before hugging both of us.

"He's growing up so fast. Sure looks like his daddy too."

"Yes he does. Poor kid's going to be devilishly handsome his whole life." Maysen says making us all laugh.

"That he will. Thank you three for coming. It was great to see you." They walk away and we continue onto the champagne table. Please let us get there this time. I'm dying of thirst.

"You two did an amazing job. It was beautiful." Oh goodness still no drink. I turn to find Aiden, Karlie and Aleah.

"Hey guys. Thank you for coming and for all your help." Tarley says as they want hugs from us.

"It was nothing. Just glad to see the last of us hitched and ready for this crazy thing called marriage." Aiden says and Karlie slugs him in the arm with a smirk. We all laugh.

"Where is Sasha?" Aleah asks and I point to where she is.

"Congrats. Enjoy the rest of your night." They walk away and we practically run for the champagne.

"Oh my goodness I didn't think I would ever get a drink again." I say just as Austin and Leah appear in front of us. I take one more quick drink before they start talking.

"That's the worst. Everyone wants to talk but you only want food and something to drink." We all laugh as Austin calls us out.

"We have been trying to get over here for an hour!"

"Congratulations, it turned out gorgeous." Leah says as she hugs us.

"Thank you for doing such an amazing job on the centerpieces and the bouquets."

"It was no big deal. We love doing them. Adalynn helped with Sasha and Arianna's bouquets. She felt so big helping."

"Tell her she did an excellent job. Where is she?"

"She's asleep in Mom's arms right now. I think my parents are getting ready to take all the kids to their house and put them to bed."

"It is pretty late and it has been such a big day for all of us."

"See you later." They wave goodbye and we both drink another glass of champagne.

Ella Mae steps up in front of us with Zandra's dad whom she has been spending a lot of time with since his latest divorce.

"It warms my heart to see you two so happy and in love. You deserve nothing but the best. Love you two as if you were my own." She hugs both of us at the same time and we smile.

"Thank you for all you have done and continue to do. It means the world to us." She squeezes our hands and walks away looping her arm in Mr. Carpenter's.

"It's nice to see her not so lonely too." Tarley says and I nod in agreement. It sure is. The last couple you would expect but if she's happy then that's all that matters.

"Well, I think I'm the last of the well-wishers. After me, you two are free to leave and go eat." Aaron says with a smile.

"Good grief we are starving and dying of thirst." Tarley says and we all chuckle.

"Aaron thank you for everything you have done for me and for us." I hug him and feel tears start to form.

"No crying. You mean the world to me and I'm so happy you found each other. Who knew me losing everything would lead to three marriages and happy endings."

"True. Carter would probably have never grown into who he is without your job and his obsession with me. You wouldn't have found Amie and I would never have come to this small town to find Tarley."

"The Lord works in mysterious ways. Anyway, congrats and now you two get out of here. Sasha went with Mom and Dad. You're free. Go enjoy the first night as husband and wife."

Tarley and I run for the car as our friends cheer and blow bubbles towards us. I look back before getting in the car and see all of them lined up with smiles on their faces.

"Thank you Lord for these wonderful people, and my amazing husband." I wave one more time and we pull away.

We all have such bright futures ahead of us with Colvin as our home.

Made in the USA
Middletown, DE
03 December 2024

66038593R00126